Redemption

....

By Shelley Shepard Gray

REDEMPTION

··

SHELLEY SHEPARD GRAY

AVON
INSPIRE
IMPULSE
An Imprint of HarperCollins Publishers

Excerpt from *Hopeful* copyright © 2014 by Shelley Shepard Gray.

EPub Edition FEBRUARY 2014 ISBN: 9780062292346

Print Edition ISBN: 9780062292353

10 9 8 7 6 5 4 3 2

The Lord is close to the brokenhearted; he
rescues those whose spirits are crushed.

PSALM 34:18

Hope is the power that gives a
person confidence to try.

AMISH PROVERB

One

·········

The Return

Holmes County, Ohio
October 1866

SOMEONE WAS IN her barn.

Under the pale light of a full moon, Sarah Ropp stood on the threshold of her back door and watched the flash of light that flitted through the slats of the barn's siding like a hummingbird. Whoever was there obviously held a candle and was walking back and forth.

Or was, perhaps, searching?

The lump that had settled at the base of her throat fell to her stomach as fear reverberated through every last nerve. What if someone found the small amount of potatoes and carrots she'd carefully hidden away? Even the thought of losing her last bit of security scared her terribly.

That fear in itself was truly a little surprising. She'd begun to hide root vegetables in a small wooden crate in the barn after a band of soldiers had come through the previous fall and taken almost everything she'd had. Now that the war was over, she knew keeping food hidden away was irrational.

But memories of being alone, helpless, and hungry were embedded in her brain.

Three years ago, Daniel had gone to war and she'd been left to take care of the farm by herself. It hadn't been easy, and on many days, she wasn't certain if she was faring well or not. Most of the time she feared not.

But those concerns had to be tackled another day.

For now, she had to determine who was in her barn, and hope he or she didn't accidentally set fire to anything while inside, exploring.

As the tiny light continued to flicker through the slats, she heard Mabel, her elderly dapple gray mare, snort in annoyance at the disturbance.

For some reason, that made her breathe easier. If the animals were afraid, they would be far more agitated. Perhaps it was merely some poor soul looking for shelter. Folks were desperate these days, and she didn't blame them, but that didn't necessarily mean she was all right with them taking shelter in her barn without permission.

That, of course, shamed her. It wasn't the Amish way to be so unwelcoming or unforgiving toward her fellow man. A better woman would remember that all her belongings were the Lord's first. She should want to share that crate of food.

She should want to reach out to men and women in worse shape than herself.

Unfortunately, she just wanted the intruder to leave.

"Which just goes to show how much you've changed, Sarah," she murmured under her breath. "You've become a stranger to yourself. You've become so alone and lonely that it's a wonder you remember who you are when you awaken in the morning."

As the words reverberated in her heart, that same desperate feeling she'd hugged close ever since Daniel had gone reared up again. The truth was, she doubted she'd ever be the woman she once was.

Still, that light continued to bob between the barn's wooden slats. As if the Lord had grown tired of her hesitancy, the wind picked up, flattening her dress's gray skirts against her body. For a split second, she gripped the door frame tightly, then let go.

After months and months of standing in the dark, it was time to move forward. She picked up her heaviest cast-iron frying pan from its usual spot next to the door. It wasn't much of a weapon, but it was all she had. Daniel had taken their shotgun when he'd joined the war.

Cold dirt met the pads of her feet as she stepped forward, making her pause and almost turn back to slip on her boots. But she knew herself well enough to know that if she went back in the house, she wouldn't come out again.

She kept walking.

Glanced at the pan she gripped. She doubted it would

be much help if the intruder was a dangerous man intent on doing her harm.

But in a way, that was nothing new. In many ways, she'd been a victim of her circumstances for years now. She was an Amish widow living on her own, practically shunned by the rest of her community because her husband had decided to fight in the War Between the States.

After two years of receiving hastily written missives detailing prideful accounts of things he should not have been doing in the first place, she'd found his name on the published lists of the deceased. Though she didn't necessarily miss him, she missed everything that could have been. If he'd lived, they could have had children, maybe. Perhaps, over time, they might have even grown to live in peace together.

But that hadn't happened. When he'd left, she'd been forced to face the rest of their church community by herself. Most had thought Daniel never should have gotten involved in the Englischers' battles. She'd privately agreed.

But she'd also been secretly glad he'd left.

Never had Sarah believed that he'd deserved to die, but he had been a difficult man to please. Most had known it. Since his death, most also expected her to live the rest of her life as his grieving widow.

But like the small amount of food that she'd carefully hidden in the barn, she also had dark secrets to guard. The darkest of which was that, in private, her husband had been a cruel, hard man. So much so that she'd feared his return. She'd feared that spending years fighting side by side with the English—firing weapons, and being among violence and depravity—would only make his dark demons worse.

As her steps quickened, the wind gusted again and she faltered against its strength.

It was time to gather her courage and investigate. "Got, stay with me, wouldja?" she whispered to the darkness. "I need your strength, for I'm sorely afraid that the last of mine was long used up."

Melting into the shadows of a bright harvest moon, she continued her journey. The ground was already covered with morning frost; the icy patches made her legs tremble as the cold settled inside her skin.

And still she walked.

If the person inside was a killer, then what would be would be. The Lord was in charge of them all.

As stealthily as she was able, Sarah opened the door. The familiar heady smell of hay and horse surrounded her, easing her frayed nerves. But she sensed uneasiness, too, from Mabel.

The mare whickered in her direction.

The noise brought the intruder out of the shadows.

She barely had time to sense that he was large, clad in rough clothes. He had a dark beard. And a face that was at once harshly familiar and terribly strange. Suddenly, the match he'd been holding flickered out, shrouding them in darkness.

For a split second, she gripped the pan . . . though to do what with it, she didn't know. Carefully, she set it on the floor, then stepped forward.

It seemed that the time for hiding had long since passed. Forcing herself to talk through her parched mouth, she called out, "Do you need help, sir? Do you seek aid?"

Only silence met her inquiry.

Her breath hitched as she waited and worried. Kept her eyes directly on the shadowed form next to Mabel. "Can you hear me?" she said, a little bit louder. Finally, she reverted to her comfortable Pennsylvania Dutch. "Can you understand me? Do you speak English or Deutsch?"

The span of a heartbeat passed. Another.

Her nerves frayed as her worst fears surfaced. This man was surely going to kill her after all. Obviously, he'd imagined the farm was abandoned, and she'd scared him.

Or perhaps he'd learned from the folks in the community that she was subsisting on the farm there. By herself. Some of the soldiers touring the area had shown her that some men preyed on weaker souls.

Perhaps that was what this man was doing.

She started to tremble. Closed her eyes and quickly asked the Lord to forgive her for her sins. The unmistakable sound of a match scratching against a post caused her to tremble. She opened her eyes just as he lit a candle.

The man raised his hand. She watched how the flame rose inch by inch, illuminating the man's torso, shoulders, neck. His clothes were frayed and grayish-blue. Many times mended. Worn.

Then the flame reached his face. All at once, she spied scarred and puckered skin covering the left side. The skin around his lips and nose looked to have been pulled tight, making his features seem distorted.

Finally, she gazed into his dark eyes. They looked haunted and desolate.

And curiously familiar.

The rest of his skin was poorly healed and full of ridges and red welts. Forcing herself, she looked at him more closely. Noticed the way he seemed to favor one leg. Noticed how his hair was shaved close to his skull . . . but looked the color of fresh pecans.

"Sarah?" he rasped. His gaze direct and solid. Burning.

She gasped as her fears turned to reality. Clasped her hands together to try to prevent them from shaking.

It seemed her husband had returned from the dead.

She wanted to deny what she saw. She wanted to separate what her heart was saying and what her brain was telling her.

"Sarah, I'm back," he said. Quietly. Not as if he antici- pated a welcome. Instead his voice was halting, as if he were mentally preparing himself for her to run.

Almost as if he expected her to fear him. Only that made her believe what her eyes were telling her to be true.

"Daniel?" she asked. "Daniel? Is that really you?" Feeling foolish and hopeful and terribly, terribly afraid.

After another lengthy pause, he chuckled low. "I don't know whether you're happy or disappointed to see that I sur- vived."

She didn't know, either.

Seeking comfort, she found herself gripping the edges of

her apron, pulling it into her hands, feeling the soft cotton caress her skin.

He stepped forward, his gaze continually grazing her body, examining every inch. So intently, she could almost feel his touch. "Sarah," he rasped. "I never thought I'd see you again."

He almost sounded like he used to. He almost looked like he should have. But of course, this man was scarred.

But what confused her most was his manner. Gone was much of the arrogant pride. The bright physical presence that had always scared her.

Now, for some reason, he seemed kinder. Or, perhaps, more calculated? Daniel had often played a part, becoming the caring husband when others were in sight, only to mock her reactions when they were alone again.

Was that what he was doing now? Or had he changed?

Was it even of any significance? All that mattered was that he was now back and her life was no longer her own.

He would make sure of that.

As his flame continued to illuminate all the changes, Sarah felt her knees give. Her body sagged in disbelief as she plunged into darkness.

THE WOMAN HAD fainted. Standing over her, Jonathan Scott gazed at her prone form. Tried to match everything he was seeing with everything her husband had told him about her.

It was now obvious that Daniel had left much out.

Sarah Ropp was lovely. Lovely like a society lady's thin china. Lovely like the pale pink roses littering a garden he'd once seen in Pennsylvania.

Lovely like the wishes he kept close to his chest and only prayed for when he was certain no one else was around.

In short, she was so much more than Daniel had ever revealed. It was obvious that for all of Daniel's boasting and blustering, he had never truly realized the treasure he'd had waiting for him at home.

John didn't care. Frankly, he didn't even actually want to think about Daniel ever again. All he wanted to do was savor this moment.

He'd made it to her farm. And though he'd never intended to be discovered, she'd accepted him as her man.

And that, John reflected as he bent down and carefully swung her up in his arms, was half the battle.

The horse nickered behind him as he exited the barn and kept walking toward what was surely his new home.

Two

. . . .

A Question of Conduct

"SARAH? SARAH, COME back to me now," a hoarse voice murmured in her ear, just at the periphery of her consciousness. It sounded hoarse, raspy. And almost like someone she used to know.

And because of that, it was terrifying.

Hoping to escape, though her muscles and bones didn't seem to show any signs of obeying her will, she moaned. Shied away from his scent.

The man inhaled sharply. Exhaled. Then spoke again. "Sarah, I mean you no harm. I . . . I promise you this."

Muscles tense, she waited for him to change his mind. For him to call her hateful names. It seemed that neither her body nor her mind had forgotten anything about him. But all she now felt was peace. It mingled with the blessed silence, intertwined with the faint comfort of hope. Gradually, she became aware of the pillow under her head, the warmth of the room, and a dull pounding behind her eyes.

She blinked, trying in vain to diffuse the pain. Attempting to understand what was happening.

"That's it. Easy now."

Gentle fingers brushed her cheek. The touch felt soothing yet unfamiliar. Without thinking, she turned her face into it. It had been so long since anyone had touched her with kindness, and that, combined with the rough voice sinking into her consciousness, teased her memory. Sarah knew she should know that voice but it flitted and danced just out of her reach.

"Come on, Sarah. Don't disappoint me now."

That sounded more familiar. But the tone was wrong. It sounded light, almost teasing.

Almost kind.

She blinked again. Forced her eyes to focus and her mind to clear. Little by little, she became aware that she was lying on the settee in her sparsely furnished front room . . . and that the man—Daniel—was standing over her.

Her husband had returned.

"There you are. Feel better?" he asked.

She didn't know. Panic mixed with a vague sense of wonder jolted her.

She had definitely not imagined that her husband had come back from the dead. He was here. He was real. As she stared at him, her eyes skimming the ragged jumble of scars on his left cheek and neck, she tried to find something in his face that was familiar.

She wasn't sure if she could. Had she gone crazy?

Seeing her struggle, the man knelt beside her on one knee as he reached out and brushed his fingers against her skin. "Please, don't be afraid," he murmured, his voice so unfamiliarly gentle. "Sarah, yes, that's it," he cajoled. "Wake up now. I promise, you are safe."

Safe? The descriptor wasn't right. She'd never been safe with him.

As her mind cleared, she became aware of his scent, his warmth. His broad shoulders and thick arms. Though he was very thin, he still looked strong. Her skin tingled when his fingers gently brushed back a lock of hair from her brow.

Had Daniel ever touched her this way? Even when he'd come courting? She couldn't recall.

Unable to help herself, she whimpered and shrank from him.

The man's expression turned pained. After a ragged breath, he scooted away a good foot. Now he was too far for her to feel the warm brush of his breath on her skin—but not so far as to be completely out of reach. One of his hands hovered over her own, as if he was considering touching her again.

She braced herself. While his left hand was scarred, the skin on his right hand was blotchy and heavily calloused, his nails dirty. But that wasn't what made her so nervous, of course.

After another seemingly endless second, his hand dropped to his side in defeat. "That's all right. I know how I look. I . . . I know how my skin feels. It's rough. I won't touch you again. Just . . . please. Please don't fear me."

Was that an order? Was it a plea?

Did it matter? Her head pounded again in earnest. She ached for the numbing comfort of another faint, but it looked like her body was determined to remain conscious.

At her continued silence, he leaned back a bit. Giving her more room to breathe.

And to gaze at him once again. Shamelessly, she studied his features, tried to unearth her husband in them. But like his skin, her memories were ravaged from their three-year absence. It seemed distance and time's passing had blurred the edges of her memory. Had Daniel truly looked like this man? Had she only imagined him being slimmer? His cheekbones less pronounced, his hairline a bit more receding? His brown eyes a slightly different shade?

For the first time, she wished she had a tintype of him. A black and white memento like she'd seen some of the English women carry with them.

Something to give credence to her memories.

Under her gaze, he sat stoically. Never flinching as she examined every ugly scar and wrinkle.

After several moments, in a voice that was increasingly strained, he whispered, "I know I look different."

At last she found her voice. " You do." She hesitated, not wanting to admit the truth, that his battered body and face were almost painful to look at. "Almost unrecognizable."

He looked away, as if he was embarrassed that she should be forced to look at him. "I expected you might think that." His voice raspy with emotion, he continued. "I know I was never a handsome man. Now, though? I fear I am the stuff of nightmares." Something flashed in his eyes that looked almost like humor.

"What happened? Was it a fire?"

Before her eyes, his expression turned almost blank. "*Jah*. Well, I mean, there was an explosion of some kind. But it was sudden and violent, and it gave birth to a fire in one of the tents."

"That must have been frightening."

"It was." He closed his eyes. Shook his head. "*Nee*. What I mean to say is, others have said it was a terrible thing. I don't remember much besides a loud noise and a bright light."

"What caused the explosion?"

He shrugged. "No one is real sure. Maybe some ammunition was out too close to a fire or stove?" He swallowed hard. "Next thing I remember, I was in a hospital tent in southern Pennsylvania. I was feverish for a time, had no idea where I was. Who I was. Only later did I come to find out that I was the one to survive the blaze. For some reason, the Lord saved me."

"And the others?" she asked. She didn't want to make his story more difficult, but she needed to piece all the information together in her head. "The others died?"

Discomfiture flared in his gaze. "Everyone but me. It's a hard thing to live with, Sarah, knowing that I lived while others didn't. And that so many men were taken to God's glory, not because of Confederate bullets, but because of an accident in the camp. I'll be carrying this burden for the rest of my life."

"It's a blessing you survived, though I can only imagine

the pain you've felt." She'd heard that burns like his were terribly painful.

He looked away. "It was, ah, painful. But I did survive."

She felt herself flinching again, but this time not from fear. Instead, it was from shame. It was obvious that even talking about the fire and his recuperation was difficult for him.

She needed to push away her own selfish wants and worries. Their past was just that, in the past. And while she might not have made peace with their relationship, she did know that she'd never wished him dead.

"Daniel, I am mighty glad you survived."

He said nothing, only stared at her. His gaze seemed to coax her into knowing him, into recognizing the man he was.

The man she was married to . . . and had almost been relieved to know was gone.

Desperate to make some sense of things, she said, "I didn't know you were injured."

"I know."

"What I mean is . . . I saw the name Daniel Ropp of Holmes County on the list of deceased. You were dead."

His lips twitched; well, the portion that could move. "Obviously, that information was exaggerated."

"*Nee*, I mean that I truly believed you were deceased." Was he upset with her for thinking that?

"I don't blame you for thinking I was gone forever." He lifted his head, scanning the area beyond her, his expression filled with regret.

He swallowed. "Sarah, the battlefield? It was chaotic.

Bloody." He drew in a ragged breath, as if the memory made it difficult to breathe. "Many men did die. It's understandable that some mistakes were made. In my case, the list was wrong."

"I . . . I, ah, yes, I suppose it was." With effort, she sat up. Once again the man reached out to assist her, but now that she was aware of him, his movements were far more stiff. Tentative. Now his hand merely lingered in the air—waiting for her acquiescence.

She couldn't bear to give it. Shifting, she moved as far from him as she could in that limited amount of space. The cold, awful truth was that she was as fearful of the man she remembered as she was of the man by her side.

To her surprise, instead of stiffening, he relaxed. "You know, it is all right if you don't want to accept me right away." After a pause, he added, "I didn't expect you to accept my return easily. I was gone for some time."

"A little over three years."

"Three years is longer than we were together."

"We lived together for eighteen months before that."

"Yes." His voice turned hard. "I know the kind of man I was, Sarah."

Do you? she ached to ask, but was too afraid.

If he truly was Daniel, there was a chance that this was simply an act. Perhaps he was hoping to lure her into a sense of security before he struck out again.

After all, could anyone really change all that much? Surely not even a body marked with scars could change how a person was on the inside? His constant need to keep her on edge, to be afraid.

As he gazed at her, as if waiting for her to believe that he had changed, something in his eyes faded when she said nothing.

She felt guilty, but only slightly so. If he were truly her husband, then he would understand more than anyone how he was behaving nothing like the man she'd been married to.

What was hard to come to terms with was the fact that he'd carried her to the sofa. The man she'd married would have left her on the ground. Shaken her awake roughly. Yelled at her until she'd gotten up on her own. He never would he have knelt by her side or tried to talk through things with her. Never would he have cared for her like this.

Now she was aware that he had not only laid her on the sofa, but he was kneeling at her side. Looking concerned for her welfare.

"What has happened to you?" she whispered.

He looked down at his scarred hands. "I told you. An explosion."

"No, I mean—" She stopped herself just in time. What kind of wife would only concentrate her husband's differences after more than three years of separation? What kind of woman would go out of her way to recall a man's flaws? "Never mind."

Moving to the edge of the sofa, she attempted to stand up.

This time, his hands did reach for her. His grip was gentle but sure as he kept her in place. Not painful. "Wait a moment, please. You need to take things easy. I fear you've had a terrible fright."

"I feel better now."

"Do you? Truly?"

Of course, she couldn't answer that. She honestly didn't know.

"And what about me? Do you recognize me now as your husband?"

His voice was almost taunting. Almost as if he was daring her to reject him. In good conscience, how could she?

All her life, she'd done what people had told her to do. She'd entered into the marriage because her parents had encouraged her. She'd been loyal to Daniel no matter what his treatment of her because she'd been taught that marriage was for a lifetime.

Now, even though he barely looked like the man she remembered, she couldn't escape the fact that she should stay by his side. To reject his story, to push him out of her life?

Well, it would feel as foreign to her as the idea of leaving everything she knew and moving to a city in the South.

And, after all, who else could he be? She was a poor widow with little to offer any man. If a man was going to take another's identity, surely he would have picked a more prosperous one to adopt?

"I don't know if I recognize you," she finally answered. "You look little like the man I remember."

Some of the hope dimmed in his eyes. "I see."

Breathing deep, she stepped off the precipice. "However, I can only imagine that you are my husband. For some reason, it seems that God has brought us back together. And surely that is His will?" That, she realized, she believed with her whole heart. What other reason could He have for bringing a man who looked like her husband back into her life? Who claimed to be the same man who'd spoken the same abiding vows that she had?

His shoulders relaxed. "I'm glad. I know I look like a stranger with these scars, Sarah. Truth be told, I feel like a stranger, too." His voice turned hoarse. "The battles were difficult. All of it was hard. Sometimes I fear I'll never be the man I was when I left here."

Dared she hope the change was for the better? She stared into his eyes, feeling a tiny inkling of hope eke into her heart. Making her realize that they'd both changed, physically and mentally.

Of course, Daniel's changes were obvious. But she had changed, too. She was thinner, older. More resigned, perhaps? Inside, she felt more at peace with her herself, perhaps because she'd had no choice.

She was now used to doing things her way.

What if he wanted her to go back to the way she was? Was that even possible? Could she return to being the same scared bride she'd been?

Or, she wondered, maybe she still was that same woman. She'd merely done a good job of hiding her.

He must have taken her silence as doubt, because he spoke again. "Sarah, listen. I'm not sure why the good Lord kept me alive, but He did. Perhaps one day we'll all understand why He kept me here on earth, I don't know. All I know is that I am mighty glad that I have been able to come home. I wanted to come back. Badly."

"I'm glad you survived, too, Daniel."

Relief filled his gaze. "Thank you for saying that."

Feeling too vulnerable, she shifted. "I . . . I think I'll be getting up now."

"Are you certain?"

"To be sure. I am fine. Now, what do you need? A bath? Sleep?" she asked as she got to her feet, holding on to the arm of the sofa as she attempted to get her bearings.

"Food. If you have some to spare."

Trying to remember what was in her icebox, said, "I don't have much, but I did make some bread and I think I have two eggs."

"Sarah, I'd be grateful for anything you make. Thank you."

He would be grateful? It was all she could do to tamp down a reaction. Never had Daniel thanked her for cooking him a meal.

He looked around. "It's awfully quiet around here. Why are you living alone?"

"Why would you think I wouldn't be?"

"I had thought everyone in the community would help you when I left," he said haltingly. "I thought, perhaps, someone might have even moved in with you for a spell. To help with chores."

She said nothing. The pain of the community's rejection had been hard.

His eyes narrowed. "What are you not telling me?"

"Nothing. Only that, well, many in our community began to keep their distance from me."

"They left you to fend for yourself?" She nodded, nothing more than a brief jerk of her head. Even now it was hard to admit how lonely she'd been.

He looked incredulous. "But why? Why would they do that?"

She almost didn't tell him the whole truth. After all, he seemed fragile, wary. But how could she lie? "Because they didn't believe in your fighting."

"But the church council decreed that we would send seven men."

"Not everyone agreed with the decision. You know as well as I do that most did not. The sentiment grew stronger after John and Amos died. And then Lloyd Mast perished. Many felt the Lord let them die to show His displeasure."

"The Lord doesn't harm in order to prove a point."

"To be sure, I agree. But you know that the Gospel forbids us to take the sword . . ."

"I see." But he still looked confused.

Her husband's dismay almost made her smile. Had being in a unit of men, all fighting for the same goal, made him forget what things were really like? "*Jah,*" she said simply.

He looked more confused than ever. "Who, then, has been helping you with the farm?"

"I haven't been completely forgotten. Sometimes Zeke stops by."

"Who?"

"Ezekiel Graber. Surely you remember him? He brought

me rabbit or venison a time or two. Sometimes he chopped wood."

"Who has been helping you with the animals? With the land?"

"No one." Obviously, Daniel had imagined that they'd all stayed the same while he'd changed. She'd been fighting her own battles. But while his were for everyone to see, she carried hers stoically. On the inside.

"Your letters never mentioned how alone you've been. Why didn't you tell me?"

His glare, his anger was almost comforting. But that was what she was comfortable with. She was used to his rages. His bursts of temper followed by moments of true remorse. She'd learned when to speak in half truths and when to back away.

Though he seemed a bit off, she still was determined to tread lightly. "I didn't want you to worry," she murmured. Of course the real reason was that she'd feared he would blame her.

Or worse, that he wouldn't care.

Daniel had viewed the roles in their marriage very clearly. He'd seen no reason for her to become involved in his business, and he'd certainly had never tried to become involved in hers. Actually, she couldn't even imagine how he could have helped her . . . especially from afar. Instead she would have expected him to berate her often.

After staring hard at her for almost a minute, he turned away, and started toward the kitchen. Wordlessly, she followed him.

"Where is the wood?" he bit out. His voice was so controlled, his posture so stiff, it sounded as if he was holding back his temper with effort.

And she became afraid all over again.

Warily, she pointed to the back door. "There is some chopped outside the kitchen. Just like always."

"Wood that you chopped?"

Nodding, she quickly folded her hands behind her back, embarrassed now of the thick calluses that had formed on them.

Shaking his head, he walked out, grabbed a couple of logs, then stomped back inside. Lit the stove. After a glance around the kitchen, he located a big pot and set the water to boil.

While the water heated so he could wash up, she pulled out a skillet, some cheese, and the remains of a slab of bacon, deciding to make him some eggs, bacon, bread, and cheese. It wasn't anything special, but the nutritious food would fill him up.

As she cut strips of bacon, he leaned against the wall and watched.

"You . . . you never answered me about the scars. Do . . . do they hurt, Daniel?" For some reason, she couldn't bear to think of him in constant pain.

His gaze lifted to hers. Fastened on her for a good long moment. At first she feared he wouldn't answer her. Then he slowly nodded. "All the time."

They stood there, staring at each other, circling around their past and their present. Neither fit them well.

Quickly, she cooked his meal and served it. She turned her back on him so he could eat in peace; it was painfully obvious that he was close to starving. Too hungry for table manners.

After he finished, she pulled out a few towels and a pitcher of cool water and set them on the table. "The water on the stove is hot now. I'll go in the back room so that you can get cleaned up."

"All right, but first, can I ask you something?"

"Of course."

"May I . . . may I hold you for a moment?"

In the blink of an eye, he'd had her at a disadvantage again. "What?" she asked, sure she hadn't heard him correctly.

"I've been gone from you for years, Sarah. I know things between us weren't good, but there were times when your letters were all I had to get me through. I promise I won't try anything more. But . . . don't I at least deserve that?"

Did he? Did she? All she knew was that her body was reacting of its own accord. She felt a pull toward him that she was unable to deny, and it seemed to trump all her doubts and fears.

Unable to help herself, she stepped into his arms. Braced herself for the unfamiliar.

After all, this wasn't something they'd done much. Her husband hadn't been an affectionate man. He hadn't yearned for her touch, had never sought out her company.

But as his arms curved around her, his head lowered, and she felt him breathe in her scent, she had to admit that his arms around her didn't feel terrible at all.

And, for the first time, it felt right.

Just as she let herself relax against him, he stepped away.

She noticed, to her surprise, that he looked a bit chagrined.

Almost ashamed.

But what was harder to understand were her feelings. For the first time in their married life, she'd been comforted by his touch. As they stared at each other, each of them breathing a bit too hard . . . Sarah wondered what had changed between them.

And then she wondered if she truly wanted to find out.

Three

. . . .

An Uneasy Acceptance

SARAH TOSSED AND turned for the first few hours after she went to bed. Whenever she was on the verge of falling into a deep slumber, she would wake with a start, stare at her closed bedroom door, and wish she had a lock on it. Every time the floorboards creaked or the wind shook the planks of the house, she shivered and tensed. Waiting for Daniel to enter and prove himself to be a liar . . . and prove herself a weakling for believing such lies.

When she wasn't waiting for his approach, she was pondering their latest conversation. She didn't know whether she had been more disturbed by his refusal to take her bed, insisting on sleeping in the spare room, or by her fear that he would change his mind and slip into her bed in the dead of the night.

At twenty-seven years of age, she'd assumed she was long past the point of being surprised by life. Experience had taught her that expectations were not always met. Disappointment was a wasted emotion.

And though the Lord meant well, He was more than a bit stingy with hope.

But Daniel's return had turned all that on its head. Despite all signs and hints to the contrary—the formal letter she'd received from his unit commander and his name appearing on the list of deceased—he'd returned.

And this was where the Lord seemed to enjoy teasing her the most. It seemed He'd not only decided to change Daniel on the outside, rendering him nearly unrecognizable, He'd gone and brought about even more changes to her husband's personality.

Now, instead of being worn and exhausted and bitter, Daniel had somehow become lighter in spirit. Instead of looking at her in disappointment and barely contained fury . . . her husband was gazing at her with something akin to respect and gentleness.

It was a miraculous transformation. An almost unbelievable one.

One that she dared not trust.

Fancifully, she half imagined that the scars on the outside of his body had helped to heal some of the aches and fissures in his soul. She'd never understood why a man like Daniel had been so intent on being dissatisfied with his life. She'd always believed his family to be patient and caring. They'd treated her kindly before opting to move to Lancaster County in Pennsylvania.

And the Lord certainly knew that she had tried her best to be a good wife to him.

All night, snippets of their life together flashed by in a jumble of memories. Jagged scenes filled with private pain and furious accusations. Memories of animosity and disappointment. Some stated loudly, others borne in silence.

They'd been two unhappy people pulled together by an arranged marriage born of a desire for good land and social standing. They'd lived each day bonded by irrefutable vows and poorly kept promises.

She'd survived by avoiding him as much as possible.

And Daniel? Well, he'd found the best method of freedom . . . he'd simply left. In truth, no one had been more excited about the thought of entering the war than he.

To her shame, no one had been more eager to see him go than she.

Now, as the distant horizon turned milky gray, she lay on her side wondering what the Lord intended for them both to do, when she heard him stir. She clutched her favorite worn, frayed quilt to her chest as she heard the rustle of the husk-filled mattress beneath him every time he shifted. Of him slipping on his boots. She heard the door open and shut, then open again.

And then footsteps approached the bedroom.

As his feet shuffled closer, her heart began to beat faster. Dread warred with curiosity as she waited for the door to open. One minute passed. Two.

But never did the handle turn.

Only when she heard him opening the front door again did she climb out of her bed and scramble into her dress.

Back before he'd left for the war, their roles had been firmly in place. He worked the land; she cared for the animals. He managed their money and their time. She worked to accommodate him as much as she could.

Which was why—after she'd carefully fastened her gray wool dress together, pinned up her hair, arranged her *kapp* on top of it, and at last slipped on her shoes and stockings—she was so surprised to see that he'd gone out to the barn.

After pumping some water to heat for coffee, she gazed through the kitchen windowpane and stared at a flicker of light moving through the barn's interior.

Back and forth it went, seemingly without reason.

Obviously, Daniel was looking for something that couldn't be found.

After another minute of watching the light bob and dip, she decided to go out and see what he needed. Surely he wasn't trying to milk Trudy? Trudy was temperamental on the best days.

However, when she stepped into the doorway of the barn, she realized Daniel wasn't milking at all. Instead, he was walking along the circumference of the walls, his hands stretched out flat against the planks. His posture was rigid. And from what she could see of his face, he looked full of intent.

It was a mighty strange sight, indeed.

So much so that it suspended her reverie. "What are you doing?"

His head whipped around. For a split second, his eyes were wide. Filled with apprehension.

Before they went carefully blank.

"My activities are none of your concern," he said at last.

She flinched. Stepped farther away from him.

Upon seeing her reaction, he scowled for a moment, before the muscles in his face eased and his tone turned fluid. "I'm sorry, Sarah. I didn't mean to frighten you. What I meant to say was that I thought I'd take a turn around the barn. See how things looked in the light of day."

"Oh. I see." She ached to point out that he held a candle in his hand. That the sun had barely begun its rise in the east. And that feeling planks in the wood seemed like a mighty strange way to become acquainted with anything. But she refrained. Questioning would only spur his anger.

At least, that was how it used to be.

"Is there a reason you came in here? Did you need something?"

"*Nee.* I, uh, came in here because I was curious as to what you were doing." She reached out, ran a hand along the wall. "You know, I never asked why you first went to the barn instead of to the *haus.*"

His expression turned even more remote. "As you can tell, the war changed me. I hoped walking around the barn would help me get my bearings." Looking away, he ran a hand along the barn's walls again. "I'm still trying to get used to be being back."

"I understand," she said. Though she didn't. Not really. "I mean, I'm trying to understand."

He smiled tightly. "And I am trying to adjust to being home. We simply need some time, Sarah."

She gripped a fistful of the skirt of her dress and squeezed tight. Just as she used to do when she was unsure of the state of his temper.

"Daniel, I was thinking that we should pay a call on the bishop."

"Why?"

"To let him know of your return, of course."

"What do you think he is going to say, Sarah?"

She squeezed her fist tighter. Surely causing terrible wrinkles in the fabric. "What do I think he'll say about what?"

"About my return." His brows rose. "Do you expect that he'll be mighty pleased to see me? Or, perhaps, do you think he'll be forthcoming about the community's treatment of you?"

His voice was filled with sarcasm and bitterness.

"I think our bishop will be grateful that you've returned, Daniel. I'm sure Jeremiah will."

"Jeremiah?"

"Our preacher. Don't you remember?"

He shook his head. "Oh, but of course. The names and places still get jumbled in my head."

She remembered just then that he'd said he'd lost his memory for a time. "Ah. Well, I think everyone is going to be mighty glad to see that you have returned safe and sound. That is what I think will happen."

His expression clouded again. "I think it would be best to wait before we see others. I don't want to pay a call on the bishop today."

She nodded before turning back to the house. Though she

had so many questions . . . for once there was nothing left to say.

AFTER SHARING A breakfast of cornmeal cakes slathered with butter, John loaded his shotgun, sheathed his knife, and went out to the woods. He was determined to bring back a hare or a squirrel, something for Sarah to make into stew for supper. The woman was painfully thin—it was obvious that she'd been subsisting on far too little for far too long.

She'd carefully folded her hands over her chest when he told her of his plans. "Do you think going out hunting is a *gut* idea, Daniel?"

"Why wouldn't it be?" Her nervousness surprised him. Surely she didn't believe he wasn't able to provide for her?

She worried her bottom lip. "No reason. But, um, it's just that one can get lost in the woods easily . . ."

It was almost as if she'd read his mind. He'd been hoping to make enough markers to return easily. He could only imagine that ruckus it would create if he showed up uninvited and unannounced on another person's property.

But remembering Daniel's pride—and his own self-respect—he pushed away her concerns. "I'll be fine, Sarah."

"Would you like me to come with you? I'll be quiet. I promise."

He felt so bad for her . . . and so incensed with Daniel. What kind of man ran roughshod over a beautiful, sweet woman like Sarah?

However, he was determined to keep to his plan, and to

seek a little bit of private time. "I'll be fine on my own," he said tersely.

In truth, he needed some time to himself. Every time he was around Sarah, he found himself thinking about other things than his real reason to be at the farm—and that was to locate the jar of money Daniel had bragged was hidden near the barn. Only when he found it would he be able to move on with his life. Only then would he be able to reinvent himself, and this time for good. Without that money, he was nothing but a poor man with a painful past and no future to speak of.

Now, as Sarah continued to stare at him in a troubled way, it was obvious that only a history of being derided made her hold her tongue.

"Daniel, please. Please be careful."

"I will." As an olive branch, he said, "Also, about church tomorrow, I'm thinking that you were right. It would be best if we went."

Her eyes widened. "You do?"

"*Jah*. It is time. After all, I am back, right?" He also was anxious to meet the rest of her church community, these folks who were so devout that they were willing to practically shun Sarah because they were upset about her husband's choices. He couldn't wait to look them in the eye.

"*Jah*." But she still looked so afraid of him, he wasn't sure if she was relieved or further dismayed by his proclamation. "All right, Daniel. I'll plan for us to go church tomorrow. If that is what you wish for us to do."

She was everything he had ever desired. Submissive,

gentle. Everything that he'd yearned to have. Everything he'd never imagined he'd have.

Reflecting on how she'd felt in his arms, when she'd dared to relax in his embrace for that split second, he wondered again about what kind of man Daniel Ropp had been. What kind of man mistreated a woman like her?

What kind of man put his life in jeopardy when he had her by his side?

Realizing she was staring at him, still patiently waiting for a response, he bit one out. "It is."

As he'd expected, she retreated, looking slightly chastised.

He made himself ignore his feelings of remorse. Instead, he slapped his hat back on his head, gripped his shotgun securely, and headed toward the woods. Only when he was out of sight did he lean against the trunk of an old elm, exhale slowly, and dare to face the truth:

He had become a very bad man. A terrible man.

And even though Daniel had abused and berated his wife . . . Even though he'd broken his promises about cherishing her and looking after her . . . Even though he'd even gone so far as to steal from her . . .

John was worse.

It was difficult medicine to swallow. Especially in the light of day.

Four

. . . .

The Celebration

"TODAY IS THE day," Ezekiel Graber—Zeke to most everyone who counted—said to his sister Ana. "This afternoon, after services at the Millers', I'm going to ask Sarah if I can court her."

Curving his hands around his mug of hot coffee, Ana's husband, Noah, grinned. "Asking her at church is a *gut* plan. After all, she can't refuse you after praying for three hours!"

"She's not going to refuse me because she's got to realize by now how much I care for her," Zeke said with a little more confidence than he actually felt.

Ana raised her brows. "She knows?"

"*Nee*. But surely she has to guess."

"Perhaps," she agreed. "Or, perhaps not."

Zeke hated to admit it, but he feared his sister might be right.

It seemed he'd spent most of his life waiting for Sarah. For two years he'd been waiting. Sometimes patiently, sometimes not.

He didn't fault his feelings, though. At last, it was time to court Sarah Brennaman.

His admiration for Sarah had started too many days earlier to ever attempt to recall. Perhaps it had been when he'd eaten next to her one balmy spring afternoon at her parents' home. Maybe it had been years later, when they'd played side by side in a March snowstorm. They'd dodged snowballs and threw others with such force that her older brother had gotten a mouthful of snow.

Oh, but they had laughed and laughed about their victory.

All Zeke had known was that she was such a prize, it was necessary he do everything that was proper with Sarah. He needed to bide his time. Wait until the timing was right. Until she was of courting age.

Therefore, he'd been in a state of anxiousness all those years ago, when he'd waited and waited for the perfect day to approach her with his heart. He'd silently counted the days until her parents deemed her old enough for courting, planning and plotting as to how he would declare his interest. Many nights had been spent tossing and turning, imagining her reaction. Imagining how it would feel to take her out, anticipating the pride he'd feel when everyone in their valley would realize that Sarah was his.

But Daniel had been quicker.

Just two days before Zeke had knocked on her door, Daniel had paid her a call. And because Daniel Ropp was everything her parents had ever wanted, she'd soon become his only company.

Not Zeke's.

Zeke had been forced to stand off to the side while she smiled at Daniel. When Daniel had taken her on a buggy ride. When he'd begun to hover over her with a proprietary air.

Zeke had been forced to hold his tongue because that was the Amish way. They didn't gossip about each other. They didn't besmirch each other's reputation.

But Zeke had ached to. He had known from the first moment that Daniel not only didn't deserve her, but wouldn't make Sarah happy. Daniel Ropp had always been a bit too assured. A bit too rough. There had always been something about the other man which seemed a bit too worldly. A bit too crass for a gentle girl like Sarah.

So Zeke had held his tongue, but his adherence to their code of honor had brought him little besides heartache.

Soon, Daniel was accompanying her most everywhere. Most folks said their relationship was serious. He'd ached to tell her that she was making a mistake, but his conscience told him to bide his time. And his brother cautioned him to keep his silence. After all, it just wasn't done to interfere with another couple's romance.

But still, he'd waited for her to realize just what kind of man Daniel was. But she never did. Or maybe she hadn't cared.

Because all too soon, Sarah married Daniel. With their exchange of vows, they'd effectively ruined his life.

Day after day, then month after month, he'd watched her

from a distance. Watched her become smaller, paler. It was evident to everyone that the relationship was taking its toll. And though it was a sin to want to break up a marriage, he'd still found himself unable to think of anyone else but Sarah.

But though they were friends, she'd never uttered a complaint, only held the faint echo of disappointment in her eyes.

Daniel's going to war had been a blessing for her, he was sure of it. And though many in their community had shunned Sarah, disdaining her as they had disdained Daniel's decision to go, Zeke had done everything he could to keep her included in their activities.

He'd even conveniently used Daniel's absence as a reason to visit her, to help her as he could. Still, she'd remained loyal to her husband . . . and he was respectful of that.

Later, when they'd heard that Daniel had passed away, Zeke had persuaded himself to believe that the Lord had intervened. Had wanted to help Sarah escape such a terrible situation, and maybe, possibly, He'd felt for Zeke, and had wanted to answer his prayers, too.

Weeks and weeks went by. Then months. All the while, Sarah continued to struggle, managing her small farm on her own. But now, the elders of the church were beginning to suggest that it was time for her to remarry. Because of that, Zeke knew men would soon begin calling on her. Even if they didn't desire Sarah, she was living on a parcel of valuable farmland.

And because life was too hard for a woman on her own, Zeke knew he was bound to lose her again if he tarried much longer.

"If you start courting, things are going to be a bit different around here," his sister said as she stood and carefully wrapped up the remains of their breakfast. "But I guess we'll figure out how to manage that soon enough."

"We'll make do." Or, perhaps, Sarah would want him to move to her place after they married. That would be the best thing to happen, for sure and for certain. That way Ana and Noah could continue to live on their farm.

As Ana pulled on her thick wool cloak, she looked him over. "Do you feel ready?"

"Ready as I'll ever be, I think." With effort, he attempted to tamp down his excitement.

"You have been a good and faithful friend to Sarah and to Daniel's memory. No one could ever fault your loyalty." Reaching out, she clasped his arm and squeezed his biceps gently. "It is *wonderful-gut* to see you so happy. Why, your eyes are fairly shining!"

So was his heart. In fact, he was so filled with eagerness and anticipation, Zeke felt sure that everyone in the whole church district was going to guess that he was the happiest man in the area just by glancing in his direction.

"I'm only going to talk with her. Ask if she'd like to go for a walk."

"She might not," Ana warned. "It's fairly cold out. There's frost on the ground."

"*Jah*, but the sky is blue and the sun is shining. And since I'll be with her, she'll hardly notice the frost."

When his sister giggled, he felt himself blush. Why, he sounded giddier than a schoolgirl!

Ana patted his arm as they joined Noah and started walking toward the Millers' farm. "I hope it goes well, *bruder*. I really do."

After almost an hour walk, they arrived. To his surprise, there was almost a festive atmosphere. Children were playing, ladies were all smiles, and men's voices were louder than usual. Laughter and teasing erupted every so often from the open barn doors.

Zeke raised his brows at Ana. "I wonder what is going on?"

"Most likely someone heard good news about the war," Noah murmured. "Maybe Mary heard about John Paul. I know she's been worried about the lack of letters she's received from him. Maybe he's finally on his way home. Wouldn't that be a blessing?"

"It would, indeed." Like Daniel Ropp, John Paul had volunteered to serve in the Union army. But while the other men's names had been listed as deceased, no word had been written about John. No one—not even his family—had heard from him in weeks. His parents and sisters still kept their hope alive, sure that they'd hear good news one day soon.

Though Zeke hadn't approved of the seven men's decisions to mix with the English and become involved with their fights, he certainly wished John Paul well. "Perhaps. If they heard good news, that would be wonderful indeed."

"When Lloyd Mast's name appeared on the list of deceased, I thought the lot of us were going to dissolve into a fit of tears," Ana said.

"The men should have never volunteered to serve in the first place. Though it's true we don't believe in slavery, and we want to help out our brothers in the North, we could have helped in other ways. It's not the Amish way to ever adopt violence."

"What's done is done," Noah said, clasping Zeke on the shoulder. "The men left three years ago of their own accord. You need to give up your anger about their reasons, whether they were righteous or not."

Zeke tucked his head. Noah was right. And once more, it wouldn't be doing Sarah any favors for him to be talking about how he felt about Daniel going off to war in the first place.

As they walked closer and heard even more happy chatter, Ana shook her head. "I bet it's not anything to do with the war at all. Perhaps Esther or Martha had their *bopplis*. They were due, you know."

Curiosity piqued, Zeke was happy to be sidetracked by any good news. He would welcome anything to take his mind off his nerves. Interested to be a part of it all, he led the way into the barn, only to stop abruptly the moment his eyes adjusted to the dimness.

Surely what he was seeing couldn't be right?

Ana huffed behind him as she pressed her palms around his shoulders. "Honestly, Zeke. Do ya have to always stop two steps in front of me?"

Without a word, he stepped to the side. Hardly aware of anything besides the buzzing in his ears. And the sight directly in front of him.

Sarah Ropp was standing next to a terribly scarred man. She looked anxious and worried, but resolute, too. And, to his consternation, happy.

His mouth going dry, Zeke stared. A thousand scenarios floated through his mind, but none made any sense.

Surely this stranger couldn't mean anything to her?

"Whatever could be going on?" Ana whispered.

"I have no earthly idea. And who could be that man who is keeping Sarah company?"

"I couldn't begin to guess," she murmured. "But he is Plain like us. Perhaps he is a relative or friend from Lancaster?"

The bishop walked over to him, Ana, and Noah. "Did you hear the news?" he asked, his voice lively.

"I'm sorry, but we have only just arrived, Bishop Thomas," Ana said politely. "What news do you have?"

"The best news of all," the bishop said with a bright smile. "Our son Daniel has returned."

A buzzing formed in Zeke's ears. "I'm sorry? What did you say?"

The bishop slapped him on the back. "I know, young man. It's hard to fathom, but a true testament to the power and glory of the Lord. Our son Daniel Ropp has returned to our community. Glory to our Lord!"

While Noah whistled low and Ana stood stock-still, Zeke attempted to make his mouth form words. "That . . . that is Daniel?" he murmured. "Are you sure?"

Bishop Thomas's brows snapped together. "Why would you ask such a thing?"

"It's just that it sure don't look like him."

The bishop frowned at him. "Of course it doesn't, Ezekiel. The poor man was burned something terrible. He was hurt in Pennsylvania, and was so badly injured he didn't even know who he was for a time." Sanctimoniously, he added, "It's only by the Lord's greatest blessings that he is here at all." Waving a hand through the air, he said, "Aren't you sometimes awed by our Lord's miracles? I know it is not for us to say, but it is truly evident that the good Lord has a plan for our Daniel."

Was that what it all meant? His mind was a whirl of confusion. Doing his best to control the tremor in his voice, Zeke murmured, "Wh-when did he return?"

"Two nights ago. Sarah said he showed up in the barn, a bit out of sorts." He chuckled. "Sarah shared that she was so surprised, she fainted right away." He slapped a hand against his thigh. "Only our timid Sarah would admit such a thing."

And only Bishop Thomas would share such a thing with such glee, Zeke reflected darkly, unable to stop staring at the couple. "*Jah.* I'm sure seeing Daniel returned from the dead was quite a shock."

Now, unable to stop staring at Sarah, Zeke asked, "Is she all right?"

Ana grasped his arm. "Watch yourself, Zeke."

But the bishop ignored Zeke's strangled expression. "Of course she is all right. Why wouldn't Sarah be anything but *wonderful-gut*? Her husband is back!" The bishop lowered his voice. "I'm a bit ashamed that just a few weeks ago I rode out to her *haus* and even encouraged her to think about getting married again."

"There would be no shame in that. Of course we never

imagined that the reports were false and Daniel was alive in truth," Ana pointed out.

Bishop Thomas nodded. "Of course I did not. Otherwise I would have counseled her differently." He sighed. "I was only on the Lord's errand, you know."

"The Lord's errand?"

"Indeed. He wants us all married, and especially eligible women of Sarah's age." Lowering his voice, the bishop leaned close. "I had quite a talk with her, if you want to know the truth. She said she wasn't interested in remarrying, and to my shame, I ignored her wishes."

"I'm sure you only meant the best for her."

"Indeed." He chuckled. "If you can believe it, I even talked about you, Zeke. I was so determined to find her a new mate."

As a matter of fact, he could imagine that. Very much so. He cleared his throat, preparing to say something, though what, he didn't know.

But the bishop cut off any words with a gruff laugh. "Luckily, the Lord's plan showed us the way in the end. Sarah stayed true. And now she has her just reward. Her husband has returned. Now things can go back to the way they were. It's nothing short of a miracle!"

Pain and hurting coursed through Zeke, as well as the sense that he seemed to be the only one—besides Sarah— who had been aware of just how badly she'd been treated by Daniel. And because of that, he knew that it wasn't a miracle. It wasn't anything to celebrate.

Instead, it was the worst news imaginable.

Ana gripped his arm, hard. "Zeke, get ahold of yourself!"

she hissed in his ear. "You are glaring at Sarah and Daniel. Someone is bound to notice."

He complied, but on his own time, and only after looking his fill. As if he'd sensed the gaze, Daniel lifted his head and searched the crowd. At first, he looked shocked by receiving Zeke's hard stare. His brown eyes were clear and curiously devoid of the usual pride that helped characterize the man. But then, little by little, he returned the glare.

And slowly raised a brow.

It was a challenge, and to Zeke's way of thinking, he deserved every bit of it. Yet again he had been coveting another man's wife.

Zeke turned away, shaken and ashamed. What he felt was terribly wrong. Not good.

But then, a tiny inkling of something new spurred him to look back again. Something about Daniel was different now. Whether it was the scars, the shock of seeing him again, or the fact that three years had passed, Zeke wasn't sure.

All he knew was that this change was just as hard to accept as the man's return. And the fact that once again he was going to have to resign himself to the awful truth. Sarah Ropp was still not his and she might not ever be.

THE MOMENT THE crowd of well-wishers thinned out a bit, John pulled Sarah over to the side. "Who is that man?" he whispered as soon as he was certain that they wouldn't be overheard.

Sarah turned. "Which man?"

"The man standing over by the thicket of trees. He's standing with the woman with the fair hair."

After scanning the area, Sarah smiled softly. "Daniel, surely you remember Zeke Graber. We've known him all our lives. Like younger boys always do, he was always trailing after you when we were all younger."

"Oh. Now it is coming back. When I left he hadn't quite filled out yet. And I think he's grown several inches," he added, hoping it made sense.

Sarah relaxed. "Oh, of course. I sometimes forget how people do change."

"Except for you, of course."

"What do you mean by that?"

"Only that you are still as pretty as ever," he blurted, unable to resist the temptation of coaxing a smile from her.

She blushed brightly, but kept her attention on Zeke. "In case you forgot their names, Zeke is standing with his sister Ana." She pointed to a solid-looking fellow talking with the bishop. "And that man there is Noah, Ana's husband."

"Are they close friends of yours?"

"Fairly close. Well, Zeke is, at least."

Her ready answer gave him pause, even though John knew he had no true reason to feel any jealousy or possessiveness. "What do you mean by close?"

She looked at him curiously. "Well, I mean we used to be close friends. And he has been good to me. A real good friend when you were gone."

"How so?"

"Well, some in our community weren't happy that you

had joined the infantry, you know. Because of that, sometimes they ignored me. He stood up to them."

"So he's a good man."

"*Jah.* A mighty *gut* man. And, well, I've known him a long time, since we were mere *kinner.* Why?"

John debated with himself about how much he should say. The man was obviously unhappy about his arrival, but John wasn't sure about how much he wanted to give away. He couldn't remember Daniel ever mentioning anyone called Zeke. But that didn't mean that he hadn't been an important part of Sarah's life since Daniel had departed.

It certainly wasn't worth questioning her about it. "No reason," he said. "It is only that he was looking at me like I'd done something wrong. Like I said, my memory is full of holes."

One side of her lips rose. "Don't worry, Daniel. It will all come back. You just need to give yourself time."

Still watching Zeke sending him grim looks, John said, "Now that I'm back, I hope he realizes that he won't need to look out for you as much."

She looked puzzled by his display of jealousy. "Daniel, I promise, I never betrayed you. We were close, but never in a romantic sense, if that is what you are concerned about. We were merely friends. Would you care to walk over and visit with him?"

"*Nee.*" He wasn't eager to be around anyone who might be suspicious about his identity. It was better to remain aloof. When her eyebrows rose, he gentled his tone. "I mean, I am sure that there will be plenty of time to get to know him."

"You mean reacquaint yourself with him," she corrected.

"Yes. That is exactly what I meant." Forcing a lighter expression, he said, "But that doesn't mean we should continue to stand here by our lonesome. I am anxious to renew our friendships. Come, Sarah, stay by my side, and we'll have some lunch."

"You know as well as I do that we cannot stand together right now. Perhaps you'd rather go visit with the other men by yourself?"

"Not yet." That was the last thing he wanted. He didn't trust himself to navigate the conversations without Sarah's help. But more importantly, he didn't want to leave her side. For too long, it seemed that Sarah had always been left to her own devices. Forgotten.

He definitely didn't want her to ever feel like she was forgotten again. At least, not for the short while that he was there. Once he found Daniel's money jar he was going to do the only thing that was right—leave her. Having her believe that he was her husband, risen from the dead, any longer than completely necessary seemed unreasonably cruel.

Sarah blinked. "Daniel, are you sure?"

Unwilling to let on just how nervous he was, he decided to err on the side of romance. "Of course I am sure. I don't want to leave you."

Her cheeks flushed. "I don't know how to react when you say such things."

"You don't need to know. I just want you to be yourself."

Because she looked even more flustered, he leaned closer. Closer than was seemly in public. But he was too desperate to keep her by his side. And too intent on making her realize that she was important. Worthy.

Beautiful.

"I know it ain't seemly, but be kind to a man just home from war, Sarah. Don't leave my side just yet."

She blinked. "You must know I could never refuse a request like that."

"I had hoped you could not," he murmured with a smile. "I dared to hope."

"In that case, I will stay next to you all afternoon, Daniel," she whispered. "But do not blame me if we cause talk."

"I look forward to the commotion our relationship will bring."

Five

. . . .

Excuses and Lies

A FULL WEEK had passed since they'd walked proudly through their church community, practically daring one and all to question their behavior.

It had been a difficult moment, made more so by the fact that Sarah was still secretly questioning things about her husband. It was so difficult to mesh the memories of her husband with the man who had returned from war.

She'd just mended the collar on one of Daniel's shirts when she noticed that the seams seemed a little bit worn and pulled. As if his shoulders had broadened since he'd left for his service in the infantry.

As she stared at the seams in confusion, the doubts resurfaced. It wasn't that she didn't believe this man was her husband, she did.

But all too often things didn't match up in her head. And while she'd never thought of herself as a particularly smart woman, she truly didn't understand how he'd come to be a different man in so many ways.

Frustrated with herself, she resolutely pushed her worries away. Obviously, she was making mountains out of molehills! Daniel had only been twenty-five years old when he'd left to join his infantry unit in Pennsylvania. Of course, his body would have changed in the three years since she'd seen him last, especially if he'd been in the infantry.

Besides, more than one woman of her acquaintance had revealed that her husband had grown another inch or two in his twenties.

Though it didn't make sense, most likely that was what had happened with Daniel.

But no matter, she was his wife, and that meant she needed to take care of him. Which meant, of course, that she must go measure him and make him a new and better-fitting shirt.

Since he'd told her he was going to be stacking much of the wood he had split the evening before, she called out to him from her place at their table. If he was anywhere in the vicinity, he would hear her without a problem. "Daniel?" Sarah called out. Waited a moment. When she heard nothing, she tried again. "Daniel, could ya come here for a moment, please? I've got a question for ya."

She heard footsteps, but no answer.

A little peeved, a little concerned, she walked to the door and peeked out. "Daniel, can ya hear me?"

"I heard you, and I will be there directly. But I need a moment." His voice sounded vaguely put out. Like she was interrupting an important chore.

Her first impulse was to set the shirt down and wait patiently. But as the seconds passed, she reconsidered. Surely he wouldn't mind a brief interruption? All she needed was a couple of minutes of his time so she could continue to sew while the light was good.

Decision made, Sarah walked around the corner of the house. "Daniel, I'm only trying to get your—" The last word caught on her tongue.

Because she now understood why he hadn't been answering her right away. It seemed he had been washing up.

Her feet froze. So did her eyes and mouth as she stared at her husband.

He'd been in the process of dunking his head into an old barrel of rainwater. When she startled him, he'd stood up with a start. The motion swung his chin length hair back from his face, sending streams of water rolling down his back in long trickles.

Those trickles meandered down his neck, past his bare shoulders, at last sliding down his naked torso.

Sarah blinked. She wasn't sure if she'd ever seen Daniel stripped to the waist before. He'd only come to her bed in the dark of the night, and even then she couldn't recall if he'd ever been completely unclothed.

But Daniel now, in the light of the day, took her breath away. He was more muscular than she'd realized; fine lines of muscles rippled along the lengths of his right arm and across his shoulder. What skin wasn't terribly pocked and scarred, that was.

Layers upon layers of mismatched, rough skin coated much of the left side of his body. Where the smooth parts of his skin were tanned and toned, the burned sections looked pieced together, patched almost. Angry and red. Mottled and uneven.

He looked to be in pain. Before she could stop herself, she gasped and strode forward, her hand out. "Oh, Daniel!" she cried out.

The shirt that he'd been holding in front of him floated down to rest on the top of the barrel as he backed up. "Turn around and go back inside."

For the first time since she'd made her vows to him, she refused. "*Nee*. I want to see you." When his eyes flared, she stepped forward, aching to make this all right. "I mean, I want to see all of your scars." Realizing that she was making a muddle of her good intentions, she blurted, "I mean, Daniel, pray, are you hurting?"

"No." He stood stoically, but his expression was fierce. And he was staring at her raised hand like it was a weapon aiming to cause him harm.

Slowly, she lowered her hand. But she couldn't avert her gaze. Once more, she felt it was important to keep looking at him. To let him see that she was worried, not repulsed by him. "I knew your body was scarred, but I never guessed your wounds were so encompassing."

He shrugged, obviously preferring to act like her gaze wasn't affecting him as much as it was. "How could you know?"

"I couldn't. Because you didn't tell me." She didn't even try to hide her irritation.

"What would it matter? It isn't like you could make them go away."

But it did matter to her. She wanted him to have someone in his life who understood what he'd been through. "I would have liked to have known. After all, you are my husband." Before she thought the better of it, she said, "Could ya turn around? I would like to see your back."

"Sarah—"

"Please. I just want to know, Daniel. I want to know how badly you were injured."

The glare he shot her told Sarah everything she ever needed to know about what he thought of her request. But without a word, he turned.

She'd never been so glad that God had not given man eyes in the back of his head. Because Daniel was just as terribly scarred on his back. And, she realized, there were other raised marks under his scars. Marks on the parts of his skin that were almost smooth. Marks that had been there for a very long time.

Ones that she couldn't recall ever feeling, even when she'd hugged him tight.

"Daniel, someone hurt you before that fire," she said. "Who made those marks on your back?"

He turned in a flash. Reached for his shirt, then frowned as he realized it was soaking wet. "Sarah, I'd like to finish washing now."

"I don't understand why you've been washing outside like this."

"You knew I have been bathing out here."

"*Jah*, but you've always washed up after I've gone to bed. Sometimes I've heard you pumping water and heating it. I, um, had thought that you were washing in the kitchen like I do."

"I don't mind washing outside. I'm used to it."

"Is that how you had to bathe when you served in the infantry army?"

His expression turned rueful. "We didn't get too much time to bathe, Sarah. Besides, half the time we didn't have enough water for things like that."

"How did you get those marks on your back?"

"I told you," he said with an exaggerated patience. "There was an explosion just outside our tent."

She hated to push it, but she needed to know. "*Nee*. I mean, before. How did you get the raised marks under the burns? They look like scars from a whip."

An expression that was as stark and bright as fresh pain crossed his features before he stared hard at her. "That is none of your business."

She knew he'd never mentioned them. But of course, Daniel had always visited her bed in the dark of the night and had left his nightshirt on. Never had she had an occasion to see his back unclothed.

Scrambling for a reason, she asked, "Did your father do that to you? If he did, I'm mighty surprised. He seemed like such—"

"I don't want to talk about my back," he interrupted. "Ever."

His words entered her head, but for the life of her, she couldn't resist saying all the things that he most likely didn't want to hear. "Would you like me to ask the midwife if she has any more salve on hand?"

"Midwife?" He scowled. "Sarah, what in the world are you talking about?"

"Do you not remember the widow Frances? She's the midwife, but the Lord gave her many healing talents, too. She has some salve that eases scars and the pain from scars."

The unblemished side of his lip rose a fraction. "I'm sorry, but no salve is going to help my looks."

"That wasn't what I meant. I meant it might ease your pain."

"My pain isn't unbearable."

But she remembered that first morning, he'd told her the scars did pain him.

He was hurting.

Though he'd stepped away from her, she walked a little closer. Forced herself to ignore the way his muscles tensed, as if he was preparing himself for her worst.

Hating his reaction, hating the reticence in his movements, she measured each word. Not wanting to frighten him, but not wanting anything in her heart to go unsaid. "Daniel, when you were gone, I prayed for your safety. I prayed that you would come home to our church district. I worried for you."

She swallowed hard, forcing herself to continue, even though each word was harder to admit than the next. "When we received word that you had died, I cried for you. And I prayed for your soul. Never did I realize that you were injured and alone."

"I know this. Thinking I was dead is not your fault. I've never blamed you for believing what everyone thought to be true. And to be honest? Well, it almost was true. I did almost die."

"*Nee*, let me finish." She took a deep breath. "Daniel, when you came home, when you showed up here, I was so surprised."

"I believe you were in a state of shock," he murmured.

"I was so surprised, and so confused, I don't believe I've ever truly come to terms with how badly you must have suffered. I am sorry for that."

"There is no need to apologize, Sarah. I am fine." With an impatient swipe of his wet hair, he said, "Now, could you at least tell me why you came out here in the first place?"

"Oh! I was, uh, wondering if I could measure you for a new shirt." Goodness, but that seemed like a lifetime ago.

"My shirts are fine. I mean, when they're dry . . ."

"I think they might be a little small. It's obvious that you grew a bit stronger and taller while you were a soldier."

"What do you need me to do for this measuring?"

"Nothing too difficult." She held up a small length of yarn. "All you have to do is stand still while I wrap a piece of yarn around you. I need to get your new size."

Something in his eyes shuttered. "I don't think so."

"Whyever not?"

This time, she could have sworn a light blush stained his cheeks. "Don't make me say it."

"Say what?" She was truly confused.

"That it isn't a good idea for you to touch me."

"I won't hurt your scars, Daniel. I promise, my touch would be light."

"I am sure it would. But I am not ready for that. My skin ... it isn't the same."

He was talking in circles! "But—"

"Please, Sarah. Now, is the shirt you were working on in the kitchen?"

"*Jah*. But that's what I'm trying to tell you. It's too small."

"It will be fine. Stay here and let me put it on."

"All right, Daniel."

He paused before striding past her into the house. More confused than ever, she fished the shirt out of the water barrel and walked out to the line to pin it up.

ONLY WHEN HE was behind the closed kitchen door did John feel like he could finally exhale. Never had a conversation so threatened to tie him in knots.

He'd felt like he'd been playing mental hopscotch with Sarah, deflecting her innocent questions with innocuous answers. Worse, he doubted that she had believed everything he said.

Once more, he knew he'd hurt her feelings with his refusal to let her measure him for shirts. But not only did he fear that he'd enjoy her tender touch too much, he also felt too raw inside. Too haunted by memories that had nothing to do with pretending to be Amish or reliving the first harrowing days after regaining consciousness in the field hospital.

It had much more to do with being an orphan given to a farmer and his family to be used as nothing more than an indentured servant. Supposedly, he'd been there to work for food and shelter, but that was hardly his life. He'd ended up being much less of a child and much more of a whipping post for an angry, bitter man with little money and even less faith in anything good in the world.

It had been a long time since he'd let himself remember those days, the feel of the cane snapping across his shoulder blades for yet another imagined sin.

He hated that with one small question, Sarah had brought all his carefully buried memories back to life. In seconds, his pain and shame had threatened to suffocate him. His feelings of helplessness had consumed him.

It all reminded him that he was truly nothing like her husband had ever been. Though John had never liked Daniel Ropp enough to truly call him a friend, Daniel had been a man of faith.

In addition, he'd been everything John was not. A land-owner. A husband and a farmer. He'd even believed in the Union's desire to end slavery so much that he'd gone against the tenets of his religion in order to support that cause.

John, on the other hand, had been an orphan with little self-esteem and even less in his pockets. Though he'd known enough about being owned by others to fight for the end of slavery, he'd also had far more selfish reasons to fight. For him, the war had been an opportunity to make something of himself.

And for a short time, he had gained other men's respect. He'd stopped being only the sum of his deficiencies. For a little while, he'd suddenly become more.

And now? Now he was even less than he'd ever been.

Fingering the soft cotton on his skin, he sighed. Here, even now, he was wearing another man's hand-me-down shirt. No wonder it didn't fit him well. It was very likely that it never would.

THEIR QUARREL HAD been a good thing, Sarah decided as she kneaded bread one morning a few days later. Something had happened on that afternoon, had made them on more even ground. Perhaps seeing Daniel's weaknesses had enabled her to not shy away from her own quite so much.

"Or, perhaps, at last accept my weaknesses?" she mused as she sprinkled more flour on the countertop and pressed her palms into the dough.

Yes, that was a better descriptor. She had begun to accept herself, and consequently, she'd begun to accept their shifting relationship.

She'd stopped jumping every time he entered the room. She'd stopped being afraid to voice an opinion, even if it was about the weather. Once or twice, they'd shared a smile.

And just the day before, when they'd spied a pair of deer near the yard, they'd both been transfixed by their beauty.

Only after the deer had gotten spooked and darted into the clearing did they both remember that he should have been reaching for his rifle instead of her company.

It was moments like these that made her realize how much of her newfound peace had to do with her husband's calm and careful demeanor. In many ways, he treated her like a frightened doe in the forest. His movements around her were slow and sure. His expression was continually steady and relaxed.

Because of that, she was able to spend more time with him without fear. Therefore, she had begun to notice some things about her husband that she'd never noticed before.

One was that he had now become both an early riser and a night owl. Unlike their first year of marriage together, her husband now seemed to need only the smallest amount of sleep, barely four or five hours. It seemed he was always up, either working or gazing out into a distance only he seemed able to see or recognize.

What was even more surprising was his agreeable disposition. The Daniel she'd married had been a constant mixture of moods, most of which changed and ebbed hour by hour, if not minute by minute. She'd never known what would set him off, or what would cause him to relax.

Far easier to handle, but no less confusing, were his new eating habits. Unlike before, he ate anything and everything. The Daniel she'd known had looked for flaws in almost everything she'd made. Little was ever good enough. Rarely was anything better than that.

In the days since he returned, however, Daniel had a ravenous appetite. He seemed to look forward to each meal, and would gaze at each dish as if it were something special. He took pains to let her know his appreciation, too. He would smile softly whenever he complimented a meal. Her inability to accept his thanks seemed to amuse him to no end.

For some strange reason, he no longer seemed to view all their blessings as gifts from the Lord. Instead, he seemed intent to praise her efforts. He also took much pleasure in an easy chore. Every time she was tempted to ask him about that, an old memory would surface, one that was horrific and dark. And she couldn't bear to sully their current life with things he seemed to have forgotten.

Though she probably should have, she mused as she carefully placed the dough inside the prepared pan.

Only a changed man would waste so much time doting on his wife. Or tease her so much. Or stare at her like she was someone new and previously undiscovered. Every time she caught one of his looks, he'd hold it a little longer. Making her blush. Making her fumble for the right response.

But of course, whenever she tried to do that, he would laugh, as if she'd just told a particularly funny joke. Sarah couldn't remember the last time she'd blushed so much.

But all those differences paled next to the greatest change. Simply put, Daniel had chosen not to return to her bed. From the first, he'd chosen to sleep on the sofa in the main room.

At first she'd been relieved.

Then, curious. He'd merely brushed aside her questions,

blaming his preference on the night terrors he now suffered from. He claimed he didn't want to disturb or frighten her.

The idea that he cared about her feelings was just as disturbing. From the eve of their wedding day, her husband had been intent on having a son. Few nights had ever passed without him visiting her bed.

There had been little affection and even less tenderness.

These two things together should have been enough to cause her to question him.

Surely even guns and weapons and bayonets didn't change a person's true nature? His sleeping habits? His need to have a family? Those seemed like something inherent.

But every time it was on the tip of her tongue to question him, to ask Daniel about how he needed so little sleep now, or why he now thought all food was delicious, she bit her lip. Preservation kicked in.

She was sure she was on the verge of opening a closed box full of hate and anger.

The memories were too strong to forget. And too painful to relive.

After all, if he'd changed once, he would surely change again.

But when he entered the kitchen with an egg in his hand and a bright smile on his face, she realized just how complete his transformation was. He looked handsome and happy and eager to see her.

So much so that it was almost impossible to have any doubts about a happy future with him.

She couldn't help but tease him a little. "And what do you have there, Daniel?"

"One perfect egg. Marjorie even gave it up without pecking my hand."

"Hens do lay eggs. It's what they're supposed to do."

"She hasn't been doing much of anything lately."

"That is true." She chuckled. "Marjorie is a contrary sort of chicken, I guess. I feel lucky we get any eggs at all."

"Well, we'll be blessed with her offerings today," he said with a smile. "We shall have an egg for breakfast." He handed it to her. "Could you fry it up, Sarah?"

"I will, but this will be yours, of course. Not mine."

"We'll share it. I want to share it with you." He paused, then reached out with the pad of his thumb and glided it along her cheek.

"Daniel?"

He held up his thumb. "You had a bit of flour on your cheek. It's gone now."

Her lips parted but she couldn't think of another word to say. His gaze felt too strong. Too direct. For a long moment, she stared at him, her heartbeat accelerating.

And she realized, with some alarm, that it was not fear making her pulse race. It was something new. Something different. Something other women had whispered about.

And until that very moment, something she'd always imagined had been a lie.

Six

. . . .

The Search

JOHN HAD NOW been in Holmes County—and in Sarah Ropp's life—for three weeks. During this time, he'd learned a lot more about Daniel Ropp, and about the Amish way of life Daniel had been so proud of.

At first, fitting into the Plain lifestyle had felt as tricky and dangerous as shaving for the very first time. But then, little by little, many things had become easier.

He'd gotten used to living in a closed community. He'd begun to appreciate the Amish men's humor and gentle teasing. And the acknowledgment that all gifts came from the Lord Himself.

That notion had never been one that Daniel had discussed much. John now wondered if it was because Daniel had feared it would never be understood by an outsider . . . or that Daniel hadn't necessarily believed it.

John's acceptance of such faith came as a surprise to himself. He now recognized the Lord's hand in so many things—from his meeting Daniel, to the fact that they looked much alike, to the friendship that was growing between himself and Sarah. He'd certainly never intended to become connected to Sarah or her land or her small Amish community. From the start, all he'd wanted to do was find the money that Daniel had bragged about hiding and begin his own life.

But his growing feelings for Sarah made him wonder if he could ever simply walk away from her. Singlehandedly, she'd made him believe in love and tenderness—two things he'd certainly never experienced growing up. He found himself eager for her smiles—and any opportunity to take care of her.

To his shame, he'd also become a skilled liar. Though he'd never had much to speak of, he'd imagined he possessed a certain type of dignity, or at least a character that he could be proud of.

That was no longer the case. As each day passed, he'd found himself further drawn into Daniel Ropp's life, his goals, and his dreams. The downward cycle was difficult. The more evidence he discovered about Daniel's life and his terrible treatment of his wife, the more John yearned to make amends. How that would help her in the end, he wasn't exactly sure.

Now, as the sun set in the horizon, he sat on the front steps of their rickety front porch and attempted to plan his next move.

"Ah, you're still here," Sarah said as she walked out to the porch to join him. "You've been so quiet, I wasna sure."

With effort, he controlled the tremor of longing that traveled through him whenever she was near. "I've only been looking at the sunset. It's a fair sight this evening."

Sitting by his side, she stretched out her legs. Turned her head in the direction he was looking, and sighed. "It is wondrous, for sure and certain."

He noticed she was holding her tongue and forced a chuckle. "But?"

"But, well, sometimes I still canna place the man who's sitting next to me with the one I used to live with."

They'd had this conversation before. "War changes people, Sarah. I can't help that." Ironically, he supposed it was even true for his real self, Jonathan Scott. He'd gone from a no-name orphan to a respected lieutenant. Of course, now he was a reprobate impersonating another man's life.

She looked at him curiously. "Daniel, how did it change you?"

"What do you mean?" It took everything he had not to finger the jagged scars on his face. He would have thought the changes were obvious.

"I'm not talking about your scars, though of course I know they must be a source of pain for you. I mean, going into battle, being around so many English . . . What was it like?"

This woman was so sweet. So innocent. How had she married a man like Daniel Ropp? He'd been as forceful and violent as any man John had ever met on the battlefield.

Tired of lying, of covering up too much, he said, "Being in the camps? It was like nothing I'd ever experienced before. Sometimes we'd sit around for days, weeks, even. Waiting. In its own way, it was as bad as being on the battlefield. Life is hard for a man with nothing on hand but spare time."

She turned to him, scooted a little closer. Her blue eyes widened with interest. "Waiting for what?"

He tried not to look too long at her perfect features. "Ah, we were waiting for orders. We, I mean, ah, the officers, would station their men in encampments, waiting for missives from some general. Our job was to train and rest. But, like I said, that was a difficult order to follow."

"Why?"

"The men were lonely. After a bit, they got bored. Fights broke out over things that didn't matter. And disease ran rampant. Everyone was always fighting off a dose of cholera or dysentery or influenza."

"I read a few of the newspapers from town. I heard men died of those things."

"Indeed they did." What he didn't dare tell her was that while many men died of disease from poor sanitation and unclean water, some died from their visits to hungry women who lurked by the camps. He sighed.

"Anyway, we would have days and days of training for what felt like no reason, of attempting to nurse each other when we had few skills to nurse ourselves, and then with a burst and a call, we'd be thrown into action." Remembering the blare of the bugles, the sharp commands of their captain, they would rise at dawn and start marching. Half afraid and half excited.

Because sometimes even fighting the Rebels and putting oneself at risk was a whole lot better than waiting and waiting for nothing.

"Did you get scared?"

"I did." When her eyes widened, he felt his face heat. "Are you disappointed to hear me admit it?"

She shook her head softly, a faint rose bloom lighting her cheeks. "*Nee*, Daniel. It's just that, ah, sometimes, well, you say things that I can't picture you ever saying before." She hung her head, obviously embarrassed. "That's all."

Feeling like he'd disappointed her, disappointed them both, he abruptly got to his feet. "I'm going to head to the barn. I'll be out there late, I reckon."

"Do you have to go out there again tonight?"

"I think it is best."

Tentatively, she reached for him. She pressed her hand on his arm, his scarred left arm. And to his dismay, she leaned a little closer, so close, he could smell the sweet scent of the rainwater that she used to wash her hair. "I know you want to keep us apart, that you feel like we don't really know each other anymore. But I know you're my husband."

Before he could stop himself, he curved his fingers around her palm. Letting her soft, cool skin comfort his calluses. His scars.

He knew what she was offering, of course. The right thing for his plan would probably be to accept her offer. What man who'd been away from a woman like her wouldn't have already given in to the privilege of being invited to her bed? From what John knew of Daniel, he definitely would have partaken of her charms.

But no matter how good an idea it was to accept her offer, John couldn't do it. He wanted to believe there was still a kernel of decency left inside him. He wasn't sure if there was—only the Lord would tell him for sure. But somehow he knew if he gave in to temptation, he would cross the line between everything he was and everything he'd always feared he'd become.

"Daniel? Whatever is wrong?"

"Not a thing." Choosing his words with care, he said, "Sarah, you are a beautiful woman. You are a wonderful wife. But I can't be with you. Not that way. Not yet," he said, stumbling through every word. "It wouldn't be right."

Disappointment and something akin to pain crossed her features. She pulled her hand away as if the burns had suddenly given her pain. "I see."

But of course she didn't at all.

She didn't move. Didn't say a word as he practically stomped to the barn. He hated to think that he was hurting her in any way. Even worse, he didn't want her to be embarrassed about what she'd shyly offered. But, by the same token, he knew she would be grateful that he'd declined if she ever did discover the truth.

After lighting a kerosene lamp, he entered the barn and strode to the back wall. Breathing in the musty fragrance of the wide space, he set the lamp down on the workbench and began to search in the far corner, the place where he'd stopped the night before.

There were a hundred reasons to continue the search for Daniel's money jar. He needed the money. He needed a fresh start. He needed to fulfill the promise he'd made to himself months ago when he'd first realized that he needed to take his future into his own hands.

There were more reasons than he could name, all different variations of the same thing—he needed the money.

There was no other way to get back on his feet. He knew because he'd spent many a night lying awake during the war, gazing at the stars and wondering how in the world he was ever going to survive life if he survived the war.

Before enlisting, he'd worked in the stables of a well-to-do family on the outskirts of Philadelphia. It had been the first time he'd lived anywhere for more than six months at a time. The Fishers had been decent people. They'd paid him an honest wage and had even given him two sets of clothes. It was there that he'd learned to shoot and hunt.

He'd imagined he'd live there for years in relative comfort. But then war had broken out. When Mr. Fisher and his son had enlisted, John had gone ahead and followed suit.

Then, to his great surprise, he'd become an exemplary soldier. Just before he was injured, he'd learned that both Mr. Fisher and his son had passed on. With their deaths came the realization that he was without a home yet again.

And so he took more chances in battle and fought harder.

Soon after that, Daniel had started talking to him about the money he'd hidden. With those conversations came the first glimmer of hope he'd had in ages. With money came independence and a home and a future.

Those were things he was willing to do almost anything for. Even stealing from a faceless Amish woman. He'd excused himself by reasoning that he was stealing something she didn't even know existed.

But then, of course, he'd met Sarah. And everything changed.

Sarah Ropp was like no other woman he'd ever met, and he was certain it had little to do with her being Amish and everything to do with the way she treated him.

Sarah looked at him with a combination of relief and suspicion. Gratitude and hope. She made him feel needed. Wanted. Almost worthy. And though he knew that he most definitely wasn't worthy of her trust or gratitude, he couldn't deny feeling a pull toward her.

Worse, he was beginning to fear that he was becoming dependent on her smiles. For most of his life he'd lived far from a gentle woman's touch. Only during the war, after earning other men's respect, had he begun to dream of one day having a wife, of having someone gentle and kind in his life. Someone to help him recover from old wounds and years of hurt and neglect.

It was ironic that he'd finally found the woman of his dreams, a woman he was finally worthy of . . . but she thought he was someone else entirely.

Refusing to dwell on his inadequacies any longer, he continued his search.

It was painstaking work. Daniel hadn't told him many

details about the size of the jar when they'd been huddled in deep trenches of Tennessee. Like a fool, John had never asked. So he wasn't sure if it was the size of a mason jar ... or something far smaller.

By John's way of thinking, a wad of money really didn't take up that much space.

As he hunted and sorted through old crates filled with old nails, building scraps, and twine, Daniel's voice started ringing in his ears. Reminding him of his purpose.

"A man cannot be too careful of his belongings," Daniel had intoned again and again. "It's best to trust no one when it comes to taking care of them. Otherwise, mistakes can happen. Problems can arise."

At first John had wanted to berate Daniel for his bragging, for his too-sure attitude. But then, after a time, he'd started to listen, too.

One night, after Daniel had bragged about his money jar yet again, John had given in to temptation. "Is that why you didn't tell your wife about the money? Because you were afraid she'd make a mistake with it?"

Daniel grunted. "Money is not for women to worry about, John. I would have thought even a man like you would realize that."

John had been in no hurry to admit that he'd had little to no experience with saving money. "You seem pretty certain about your views."

"I am. Women have no need to worry about money or savings. That is a man's job."

"But what if you don't come back? I'm sure your wife will

be needing the money if she will be living on her own. Or don't the Amish care about such things?"

"Of course we care about such things, but Sarah don't need the money. She's so timid and shy, she probably wouldn't even know what to do if she found my money jar."

John had wondered about that. As a man who'd grown up with next to nothing, he knew he'd never discount even a lowly ha'penny. "But how will she survive?"

Daniel waved off his concern. "Sarah don't need to worry about things like that. She's going to be nestled in the caring arms of our community, and then she'll have me caring for her needs again."

"You sound so certain." John thought about death all the time. It was impossible not to. It seemed everyone around them was at risk, either from the disease running rampant in the camps or one of the Confederates' musket balls.

"I'm certain because I have no reason not to be," Daniel replied. "Of course I am going to come back, John. The Lord wanted me to join in this fight of yours. He wouldn't have chosen me if He expected me to die."

"I hope He expects me to live, too."

Daniel had laughed at his weak attempt at levity for a good long time. "That's no way to look at things, John. You need to learn to believe in the Lord. Once you have your faith you won't worry so much about things you canna control."

John had taken Daniel's words to heart, especially the part about having faith. Times were so tough; only faith in a higher power could make a man feel better about anything they were going through.

But as far as being certain that the Lord wanted some of them to live while allowing others of them to pass away in a battle or in a sea of pain? John just couldn't wrap his mind around that. It had taken much willpower for John not to point out that each of them hoped to return. Well, those that had families to go home to.

Now, he was glad he hadn't, because Daniel then said the words that had changed his life. "If you knew my Sarah like I do, John, you would understand what I'm saying. I hid my money in a simple glass jar near our barn." His voice turning sharp, he added, "Sarah knows better than to snoop around things that are none of her business. And she certainly knows better than to do anything with the money if she did find it."

"Because?"

"Because she knows what kind of man I am," he whispered. "Because she knows for sure and for certain that my displeasure is nothing to be played with."

Now, as John sat in the empty barn, thinking about Sarah's shy offer of their marriage bed, of the way his pulse leapt whenever she was near, he realized that he was more confused than ever about everything in his life.

Except for one thing—the longer he was in her company, the more he was afraid he'd never be able to simply walk out of her life.

Her hold on him was becoming too dear.

Seven

· · · · · · · · · ·

The Discovery

THE STORM ROLLED in just after sunset and steadily intensified as the hours passed. The sky turned pitch black. Rain hammered the ground as harsh gusts of wind rattled the walls of the house. Truly it had felt as if a dark force had taken hold of her farm and was steadily punishing it through the midnight hours.

And because of all that, sleep had been elusive. After tossing and turning for hours, Sarah had finally resigned herself to simply lying in bed and listening to the cracks of thunder, wincing each time lightning illuminated the room.

Of course this wasn't the first time a storm of such magnitude had rolled through. But it was the first time that she'd realized she didn't have to face it completely by herself.

Daniel was back. And once more, it didn't seem like he would be opposed to comforting her fears. For once, he wasn't even one of her fears.

Strange, that.

Giving in to temptation, she crawled out of bed, slipped on her wrapper, and opened her door. Walked to the main room and spied the empty sofa, the pile of quilts still folded neatly on its edge.

Sleep must have eluded him, too.

As the wind rattled hard enough to shake the walls of the house, followed by a sharp crack of thunder and a flash of lightning, Sarah shivered. And in that moment, she realized how tired she'd grown of facing everything alone.

She needed to put her trust in the Lord's will in bringing Daniel back to her. Though she still didn't completely trust Daniel, she didn't fear him the way she used to, either. That had to mean something.

Hidden inside her was another yearning, for something other than security. It was the fresh awareness she felt every time he was near. Tenderness when he winced from pain. The wave of pleasure when he returned a smile.

After slipping her feet into old boots and wrapping a shawl around her head and shoulders, Sarah rushed outside to the barn. Freezing rain plastered her hair against her head before she'd taken four steps. Raindrops pelted her skin with enough force that she imagined she would be bruised come morning. Gusts pummeled her body, pushing the cotton of her nightgown and wrapper flat against her legs.

By the time she made it to the barn's entrance, she was out of breath and chilled to the bone. With a whoosh and a sigh, she pulled open the large door and pushed her way inside.

"Sarah?"

To her left, a collection of tools and nails clattered to the ground, followed by the faintest sound of cursing.

She stopped and stared, shocked by the sight before her. Daniel held a crowbar in his hands. Surrounding him were jumbled piles of tools, scraps of wood, old papers, and pieces of leather that had all been removed from the far left corner of the barn.

He glared at her as his voice turned hard. "Sarah, you'll catch your death in this weather! Why are you out of bed? What are you doing in here? It's late, you know."

She stared at him, horror-struck. Every night since his return he'd been out in the barn. But all this time she had imagined him gazing out the windows, or taking comfort in the animals' soothing proximity. Never had she imagined the sight before her.

After scowling at her again, Daniel knelt on the ground and started grabbing at the pile of tools, wood, and nails that he'd dropped. His sleeves were rolled up and his shirt was untucked. As he stood up and turned to her, she noticed that his stance was different. Suddenly, he didn't look like Daniel at all. Even the scars that she'd taken care not to notice seemed to stand out in stark relief.

It seemed everything she'd grown to trust had disappeared and been replaced by a fierce-looking man.

But even in his anger, he didn't look like the man she'd married. And yet, she realized, she wasn't afraid.

Her heartbeat quickened.

Trying to calm herself, to ease the situation, Sarah took care to keep her voice gentle. "D-Daniel, what are you doing out here? What were you doing with that tool?" Gesturing toward the piles of discarded tools, the mess of scrap wood, the spilled container of grain, she added, "Why were you pulling that peg board off the wall?"

"Ah, when the wind picked up, a few things blew down. I thought I might as well try and make some sense of it all."

She wished she could make some sense of his words. "Daniel, we both know that a strong gust of wind wouldn't have knocked everything down. And though it's not very bright in here, it's fairly obvious that you are definitely not organizing things." She took a deep breath and a step forward. Summoning all her courage, she said, "You need to tell me the truth."

Even in the darkened room, she could tell he was taken aback. After a heartbeat's time, he rasped, "Sarah, what I am doing is none of your business."

Before the war, she would have automatically retreated, fearing his anger. But time spent alone had made her braver—or maybe she was starting to trust her husband?

She took a tiny step forward, hoping he didn't notice the tremors in her hands. "What is it you are looking for?" she asked again.

"That is none of your concern."

She noticed that while his words were firm, his tone wasn't quite as sharp.

"Maybe I know where it is. I was in here quite a bit in your absence, you know."

Stepping forward, she picked up a sack that was now half empty. The grain that had once filled it now littered the floor. "Daniel, what is this? The grain here is being wasted. And mice will surely feast on the mess."

"I'll worry about the mice."

When yet another crash of lightning illuminated the barn, she met his gaze, noticed the faint gray rim around the deep brown of his irises.

Had that always been there? Had she always been so wary around him that she'd never fully met his gaze?

"Daniel, sometimes you seem so different."

He blinked. Looked away. "We've already been over this."

"I know, but sometimes, I just can't reconcile the man you are now with the one I knew."

"You mean the one you thought you knew."

"Perhaps," she murmured. But she didn't agree. Crossing to the other side of the dusty room, she picked up a small broom. "I'll clean this up. Maybe we can save some of the grain."

"Leave it alone."

"But we can't just leave it—"

"We can and we will." His voice was strained. "Listen to me, Sarah. I want you to go back to the house, dry off, and go back to sleep. Now."

She wasn't sure what propelled her, but she pulled her shoulders back and stared him down. "*Nee*, Daniel," she retorted. "I will not go back to the house. I am going to stand right in this spot until you tell me the truth about what you are doing out here in the barn."

The moment the words left her mouth, the shock of what she'd just done left her dumbfounded. Her body reacted by trembling. A cool line of sweat trickled down her spine. Never before had she ever dared to speak in such a fashion to Daniel. Not since their one and only argument during the first week of their marriage.

Warily, she stared at her husband, waited for his temper to finally erupt.

He was staring at her like she was a stranger. Seconds flickered between them fast, then slow. In uneven beats, keeping time with her erratic heartbeat. She felt like she was out of breath and panting at the same time. Fear coursed through her as she gazed at him, no longer seeing the scarred man with the hurt eye who limped in front of her.

Instead she was envisioning the man he used to be. The one with the perfect features and the kind brown eyes. The one who could smile to strangers yet raise his hand to her.

Mesmerized, she watched him step forward and raise his hand.

Her body tensed, anticipating the pain. This, she knew. With this, she was familiar.

Then, to her dismay and relief, he stopped a mere foot in front of her. His breathing seemed as labored as hers was.

She dared to lift her chin, to stare at him. But instead of seeing the flash of anger, she saw that his expression was filled with pain.

And, perhaps, disappointment?

Slowly, as if he feared she was about to bolt from the barn like a scared animal, he pulled a chunk of hair back from his face.

She exhaled. Realizing only then that he'd never intended to hurt her.

"Sarah, I will speak to you about all of this later. Tomorrow," he clarified, his voice husky. "Now is not the time. Not here, either." He ducked his head, as if he couldn't bear to look her in the eye. "Please, go."

Her pulse pounded. Her mouth went dry. Emotions warred inside her. The desire to flee was strong, but in the midst of it was another wish—a yearning to stay by his side and offer support.

That was far more confusing, far more surprising. In many ways, her desire to stay near him was more frightening than any pain he'd ever inflicted. It was unexpected. Unfamiliar.

Therefore, without another word, she rushed back outside.

And once she was away from her husband's direct gaze, she gasped and simply stood. Uncaring of the rain, she lifted her head to the heavens and closed her eyes and let the raindrops pelt her skin, splash against her eyelashes, her cheeks. The wind blew her skirts close to her body, pushed against her skin, almost knocked her down. But still she stood, almost as if she needed to feel the elements, almost needed to feel the evidence of something far stronger than herself.

When she finally got her bearings, Sarah strode into the house, but she didn't feel the cold, didn't feel chilled, didn't care how wet she was.

After lighting a candle, she went through the front room, into her bedroom, stripping off her boots, her shawl, her *kapp* as she went. Stood next to her bed, tore off her nightgown.

And stood, almost naked. Almost bare. Shivering in the dark. She wrapped her arms around herself and at last steeled herself to the new truth. To *her* new truth.

And with that new truth came a curious sense of peace. She hadn't been addled, hadn't been so overcome that she'd forgotten the most basic things about Daniel Ropp. If she knew anything, it was that the man she'd married wouldn't have been looting his barn in the middle of the night. He wouldn't have allowed a single speck of grain to fall to the floor, unaccounted for.

He wouldn't have rolled up his sleeves and allowed her to see the scars on his arm without an ounce of shame.

He would never have listened to her demands.

He wouldn't have allowed her to raise her voice at him.

He would never have stopped himself from hurting her.

And he would have absolutely never held himself in control before quietly telling her to go back to the house.

At last, she knew what the Lord had known all along.

The man in her barn might answer to Daniel, might want her to believe he was Daniel. But he was assuredly *not* Daniel Ropp. That she now knew without a shred of doubt.

All this time, she'd been living with a stranger.

A shiver ran through her. With shaking hands, she pulled on another nightgown over her head, crawled under the covers, lit a fresh candle, and waited.

Eight

· · · · · · · · · ·

The Confession

OUTSIDE, THE STORM continued. The door that Sarah had run through swung haphazardly on its hinge, squeaking from the effort. The dust and dirt surrounding John grew moist from the raindrops blowing in through the door's gap, making the air damp. Cloying.

It was a perfect mate to the complete disarray of items littering the floor.

John rubbed his arms, attempted to breathe deeply. Inwardly, he groaned.

Without a doubt, the cluttered barn had become a metaphor for the mess his life had become. And he? He felt just as useless. How else could he describe the sad, vacant feeling that had consumed him as he'd watched Sarah run away?

Picking up the lantern, John turned away from the search,

choosing instead to look for someone who had become more precious than a hidden container of money. Sarah.

How had that happened? When he'd first devised his plan he hadn't thought much about Daniel's widow. He'd hoped to simply steal Daniel's private stash and leave with Sarah none the wiser.

And if they had happened to meet? That was when his likeness to Daniel was going to come into play. He would pretend to be her husband for mere days—until he had located the money.

He'd naively assumed that Sarah would be at the very most a minor, temporary barrier keeping him from what he wanted. He had planned to lie to her and keep as distant as possible. And then leave in the middle of the night, much like the way he'd arrived.

Now he wondered how he could have ever been so shortsighted. Nothing about his feelings for her was simple and nothing about the knowledge that he'd eventually leave her gave him any sense of peace.

Still contemplating everything that had happened—and the unexpected effect she had on him—he leaned against the open doorway of the barn and watched the shadows cast by the faint flickering of her candle make its way through the house. The illumination practically begged his eyes to follow her movements into the kitchen and beyond to the small bedroom.

Through the curtained windows, he watched the blurred shadows of her movements, watched her change out of her wet gown into something dry. As each second passed, he felt like more of a fraud. More of a disappointment to himself.

No man should be filled with so many lies.

Tomorrow, he decided, would be the day. Tomorrow he would go to Sarah and attempt to explain himself. Being Sarah, she would undoubtedly listen patiently, looking at him in that calm and careful way of hers. Then, in short order, he would summon the courage to tell her all his secrets.

Perhaps she wouldn't erupt into tears and anger before he finished.

Maybe she would believe him.

Who knew? Maybe, somehow, she would even find it in her heart to not make him leave that very moment. Maybe she'd say that she could almost understand. That she could see why a man like him had chosen the path he had. And if that happened, he knew he would find redemption for his sins. Maybe even the blessed peace of freedom.

Oh, he didn't imagine that she would forgive him. He didn't deserve that. But he hoped they could come up with something to help her regain her dignity when she explained that she was all alone again. Maybe she could tell her community that he'd gone mad from the ugliness of his scars? Or, perhaps, that he'd suffered too much anger and fear from his time at the battlefield and it had altered him?

That wouldn't be a complete fabrication. He did, indeed, fight going to sleep, dreading the dreams that haunted his very being, the images that reappeared in his head and heart. Reminding him that no matter how hard he attempted to forget the past, it was always there, always lurking in his periphery.

All he had to do now was wait for her candle to extinguish. Wait for her to fall asleep so he could enter the house without fear that she would pester him with yet another question he couldn't easily answer.

With his eyes still trained on the faint light shining through the window, he devised his plan, formulated the conversation in his head. How he would take everything one step at a time. How he would carefully lay out his reasons and offer no excuses. He could almost see them having the discussion. Almost as if he had a stack of daguerreotypes before his eyes and they flipped through in slow motion.

As the seconds passed and the light still didn't disappear, his thoughts turned away from the future and settled back to the present.

And he began to worry.

What was keeping her awake? Was it the smattering of raindrops on the roof of the house? The wind that still hadn't abated?

Or were her thoughts filled with more personal concerns? Was Sarah worried about him? Was she, too, haunted by regrets and loss?

Or had she fallen asleep with the candle burning?

That seemed a more fitting scenario, though it didn't make him feel any better. If she'd fallen asleep with the candle burning, he was going to have to enter her bedroom and extinguish it. And that, of course, would bring forth a whole host of new worries and discomforts.

But surely she wouldn't have done anything so foolhardy?

After he watched for another ten minutes or so, true panic set in. Something had to be wrong. If he'd learned anything about Sarah Ropp, it was that she was a woman of habit. She liked toast with a thick pat of butter in the morning. She enjoyed sweets in the afternoon. She was altogether neat and organized. And calm, though a hint of sadness always seemed to envelop her. She also woke at the same time each day . . . and went to sleep the same time each evening.

For her to venture out to the barn and search for him was noteworthy. For her to still be awake for so long in the middle of the night was alarming.

He closed the wide doors of the barn, then walked to the house, stopping every few steps to look at the bedroom window. Checking to see if the light was still burning.

When he entered the kitchen, he extinguished the lantern, choosing to let the faint flicker of candlelight shining through the slim gap under the bedroom door guide him. But when he stood at her doorway, he wondered if he was making a terrible mistake.

It seemed an inexcusable invasion of her privacy to open her door uninvited. To enter her bedroom, pretending to have that right, when tomorrow they would both know he'd never had it to begin with.

Gazing at the handle, he wondered if he had finally crossed the line between selfishness and despair, and on into a darker territory. Maybe his desperate need to form a bond with someone had finally ruined the last bit of decency he possessed. All his life, people had told him that he was worthless, not good enough. When he'd been so badly burned, he'd overheard more than one nurse proclaim that he would have been better off dead.

Perhaps they were right. He wasn't much. He never had been. However, Sarah's safety couldn't be ignored. If he gave way to his fears and never opened the door, never checked on her, and something happened to her? Well, he would finally realize that everyone had been right, after all. He was unworthy of life on this earth.

He made a quick plan. He would turn the knob, pick up the candle, quickly take it out of her room, and close the door again. At the most, his raid would take a mere ten seconds, less if he kept his gaze averted and didn't give in to the temptation to watch her sleep.

Steeling himself for whatever he found, John opened the door and finally stepped inside.

The bedroom was cool. Muslin curtains covered the window. The room smelled of lavender and other herbs, and that strange, elusive scent that women had, of cotton and rose and everything tender. The things that men used to talk about on the battlefield.

Finally, he faced the bed, ready to extinguish the candle and make a hasty retreat.

Except he drew up short, seeing her sitting on the edge of the bed, dressed in a voluminous white cotton nightgown. Her usual head covering was gone and her hair hung loosely down her back.

And just like that, his mouth went dry. Her hair, a golden brown falling in waves past her shoulders, was glorious, transforming her from merely lovely to exceptionally beautiful.

Making him realize all he was losing—not that she'd ever truly been his, except in his dreams.

Sarah was staring at him, her blue eyes sharp. Assessing.

Obviously, she'd been waiting for him to enter. It seemed she must have known that he'd stood outside her door for five long minutes like a coward.

He measured her expression and was relieved to see that it held no fear. At least she no longer looked like she expected him to hurt her.

"You're still up," he said.

"*Jah*." Her gaze was fixated on his own. "I found myself unable to sleep. And then I realized you were standing outside my door."

"I, um, was trying to find the nerve to enter."

"I figured as much."

"Oh?"

"Why have you come in?" Her expression was solemn. Curious, not frightened.

And though she didn't seemed pleased that he was in her room, she didn't seem bothered by it, either.

Like a fool, he gripped at the door frame, unsure what to do. Did he dare step forward? Retreat? Look at her? Look at a spot on the wall above her head? He shook his head, disgusted with himself. In the service of a grateful nation, he'd risen through the ranks as a lieutenant. He'd become an officer through bravery and determination.

But in this moment, he couldn't find a way to speak to this woman in the dead of the night.

She'd become too important to him, and now he knew he had too much to lose. If he ruined this moment with the wrong words, he'd lose everything: a home, a chance for happiness. Her.

He felt tongue-tied and embarrassed. And, for the first time in recent memory, frightened.

Deciding it was best to explain himself, he murmured, "I saw your candle burning. I . . . I thought you had gone back to sleep and had forgotten it. I opened the door only to extinguish it."

She tilted her head as she continued to stare. "So you were concerned about a fire."

The very fact that it was a statement concerned him. "Yes."

"Obviously, your concern was unfounded."

"Yes. Ah. Thank goodness." With effort, he lifted his gaze and concentrated on keeping it trained to the wall. That was what a gentleman would do.

But obviously he was no gentleman. It was as much of a figment of his imagination as his hope for willpower. Yes, it seemed both had abandoned him, along with the last dregs of his honor.

Sarah continued to say nothing. Merely sat still and straight. Watching him.

Before long, he found himself darting glances everywhere in the room like an insect caught in a jar. Looking anywhere but directly at her. Though was he more afraid to view her in her prim white nightgown, or to see the look of unease in her eyes?

"I found I am unable to sleep," she said at last.

"I am sorry to hear that. The storm, it is a frightful one. To be sure. But it will pass, it always does." He ran a weary hand across his brow. Prepared to step backward and at last leave their conversation. Leave the room.

"It wasn't the storm. I fear it has something to do with your presence in the house."

He couldn't help but raise his brows at that. "My presence? Forgive me, but I don't quite understand what you are referring to."

"*Jah.* I fear I am unable to fall asleep in the company of a stranger."

He felt like he'd been sideswiped. "Pardon?"

She coughed delicately. "Come now, *Daniel.* Isn't it now time we were honest with each other? Oh, forgive me, I misspoke. Isn't it time that you were honest with me, and I was honest with myself?"

This time, he did back up. He couldn't help himself. Neither could he continue to look anywhere but at her. But the glare that greeted him nearly took his breath away. He'd honestly never imagined that she could look like the way she did. Or that she could speak so bitterly. "I fear I am not following . . ."

"No?" she snapped. "Then pray allow me to speak more plainly. You might be many things, sir. You might have been a soldier in the war—"

"I was," he interrupted, unable to remain silent about the only thing he was proud of.

"You might even be Amish, though I sincerely doubt you were ever Plain."

He ached. "Sarah—" Tried to refute her statements.

"You, sir, might have even been a good man. Perhaps you still are, at least in your own, hopelessly twisted way."

He swallowed.

"But there is one thing you most definitely are not. You are not Daniel Ropp. You are not my husband. I know this to be true to the depths of my soul."

He was so taken aback he had no recourse but to continue to play dumb. "What has precipitated this?"

"I am not answering another question until you answer me. Who are you?" Her voice broke off, at last revealing the extent of her apprehension. "Who are you, really?"

Each of her words had felt like a pinch. Each one had been disappointing but not completely painful. But together? Her small speech had packed a powerful punch. Almost debilitating. Her bravery stripped him bare.

And made him do the very thing he knew to be right. "My name is Jonathan Scott," he muttered at last.

And this time, when he dared look at her, his heart nearly wept.

Sarah Ropp, his make-believe wife, had turned deathly pale.

Nine

. . . .

The Apology

AS SHE STARED at him, the expression in her eyes a terrible combination of disbelief and hurt, John wondered if he should simply step away. Surely Sarah needed time and space to come to terms with all that he'd told her. Besides, there really was little he could offer her besides his apology.

And what could a few well-chosen words do, anyway? He could think of no excuse that wasn't ineffectual, no words that would be anything but inadequate.

He really had done nothing but take a bad situation and make things worse. He saw no way to make things better between them. It was impossible to erase the past.

Yet, when he looked at the way she was holding herself together through pure force of will, the way she looked so devastated and desolate, he knew he couldn't leave. Stepping back and leaving her alone would be an almost physical impossibility.

Instead, he gave voice to the most inane question in the world. "Are you all right?"

She raised her chin and stared at him as if she'd never seen someone like him. As if he was a beetle crawling across his floor. "*Nee*," she murmured.

Which made him feel just a little more despicable.

When she turned from him to lie on her side, wrapping her arms around her middle as if to comfort herself, he knew he must do something.

Feeling grim, John picked up one of the quilts from the edge of her bed, carefully wrapped it around Sarah's trembling body, then lifted her into his arms. They needed to talk, and doing so in her bedroom would only make matters worse.

She didn't struggle as he strode from the room.

Actually, Sarah showed almost no response, merely resting her head against his chest. Almost as if she no longer had the will to fight him.

He gritted his teeth as his apprehension grew. Growing up the way he had, he knew next to nothing about women's delicate constitutions. But he was fairly certain that gently bred women who received terrible frights needed to be tended to with care.

He placed her on the sofa, taking care to cover her more securely, before putting the kettle on in the kitchen. "I'm going to make you some tea," he called out as he reached for her favorite ceramic mug. "Some peppermint tea. That's your favorite, right? Then, we're going to talk."

She said nothing, only stared at him with wide eyes as he clattered around the room like a bull in a china shop. Somehow he managed to find her peppermint tea leaves. He steeped them in the hot water, then with a small sense of triumph, he brought her a fortifying cup of steaming tea.

After she merely stared at it, he pressed it into her hands. "Sip," he ordered. Just as if he was dispensing medicine instead of comfort. "This should help you get your bearings again."

She looked dubious, but did as he bid. After a few more sips, he sat beside her. Close enough to grasp the cup from her hands if it slipped through her fingers, far enough away that he hoped she wouldn't be concerned.

When she got some color back in her cheeks, Sarah leaned forward and carefully set the mug on the small table in front of them. And, at last, spoke. "Explain yourself."

Tossing all his prepared scripts out the proverbial window, John rested his elbows on his knees and started talking. Hoping that the Lord would give him the right words to say before she kicked him from her house in the middle of the night.

"Like I said, my name is Jonathan Scott. John to all who know me. And yes, I was a soldier in the war. I was a lieutenant." Even though that surely meant nothing to her, he let his pride talk. "I started out as just a foot soldier but before long I began rising through the ranks. I . . . I was a good soldier."

She blinked, seeming to turn over the idea that there was a chance he was better than she'd imagined. "What about everything else, John?"

"I am not Amish. In fact, I know little about your religion. Little about being Plain."

"And?"

He closed his eyes, prayed for strength, then remembered that he didn't deserve answers to any prayers. "And, most importantly to you, to us . . . I am not your husband." Feeling wave after wave of shame wash over him, he continued his explanation, though he assumed it was unnecessary. "I have been deceiving you."

"Where is Daniel?" Sarah whispered, gripping her mug once again. "Is he truly dead?"

There was no way to make the truth easier to bear. "I am afraid he truly is."

She closed her eyes. Slumped. He scooted closer to her, worried she was on the verge of collapsing. But she held herself together. She grasped the ends of the quilt more closely around her body, covering herself so completely that only her head and neck remained visible to him.

"What may I do for you?" he asked, feeling suspiciously overcome with inadequacy. After all, what *hadn't* he done to her?

The look she cast his way was filled with pure loathing. "I fear you have almost, at long last, rendered me speechless."

"I realize that this has come as a bit of a shock. I am sure you are overcome."

"*Jah*." With a little tug, she arranged the quilt around her more securely. "Tonight's events have been quite a shock. *You* have been a bit of a shock, Jonathan Scott."

Her voice was so bitter, her expression so desolate, he did

the very thing he had earlier hoped to avoid. "Do you wish me to leave? I can be out of here within a few minutes."

"*Nee.*"

"Sure?"

"I don't want you to leave. Not yet."

"All right. I will leave in the morning."

She stared at him for what felt like an eternity, but then to his consternation, she stood up, grabbed her flickering candle, and strode to the kitchen. The quilt he'd wrapped so carefully around her—the one she'd just held to herself—lay forgotten on the sofa.

At her mercy, he followed. "I owe you an explanation. But it is late. Perhaps it would be best done in the morning before I take my leave?"

She gripped the edge of her counter. "You are now concerned for my welfare? After everything you have done?"

She was right.

She deserved every explanation, just as he deserved none. It didn't matter what time in the morning it was or how distraught she seemed to be. Or how shamed he was.

Nothing mattered anymore but the truth. And so, because he truly had no choice, he began talking again.

"I first met your husband, Daniel, a whole year after he entered the war. As I said, I had risen through the ranks, and was asked by my major to join Daniel's unit." Feeling his cheeks heat, he said, "I had some experience in fighting the Confederates along the rivers. And I was adept at keeping order in the ranks."

"And?" Sarah murmured.

Not trusting himself to look at her, he kept his eyes averted. "By the time Daniel and I first met, he had assimilated into the ranks quite well. He was tough. Strong. And never seemed to get bored or depressed like so many other men. As a matter of fact, I would have never realized he was Amish until I heard the slight intonation of his voice. He fit right in with rest of us. He was hardened and battle-weary. And hungry for more. He was a good soldier, Sarah."

The muscles in her throat tightened. "That was what I feared."

John was at a loss, but continued on. He wasn't sure what to say but he was starting to understand that nothing was going to be helpful for her.

Therefore, he continued to tell the truth, even though the story wasn't pretty and the words were painful. "For all that, Daniel, ah, wasn't well liked. Men in the ranks didn't entirely trust him. They didn't fear him, but it was as if all that was honorable had gone missing from his character.

"When we first went into battle, I saw what the other men had commented on for myself. Daniel seemed to have lost a bit of his humanity. He began to look at those Johnny Rebs as something less than human . . ." He let his voice drift. Though he was determined to tell her the truth, there were some things a woman never needed to know about what happened in the midst of a hard-won battle.

And though he'd already said many unfavorable things about Daniel Ropp's character, he wasn't prepared for Sarah to ever find out just how dishonorably her husband had fought.

"Sarah, I am not sure if you want to know more? War is not an easy thing to describe."

"I want to know everything, Jonathan Scott."

"All right." He leaned back against the counter, resting his elbows on the wood planks. "Well, within time, I was his commanding officer, such that I was. His lieutenant. About a month after I arrived, we marched to the rural hills and valleys of Pennsylvania. Near the rivers."

"Because that's where you had experience," she interjected, reminding him of how much he'd already told her.

"Yes. And because that was where we had heard the Rebs were gathering." Remembering the heat, the flies, the sickness that had decimated their ranks, he grimaced. "It was, ah, a difficult location. Our captain had us build trenches and settle in. Wait." He lifted his head, hoping to find a way to make her understand how those days were.

Those long, uncomfortable, boring days. When their clothes felt both too stifling and too thin. When their skin had itched and their hair felt full of vermin and he would have given a year of his life just to feel clean again.

"We had too much time on our hands. Or maybe it was just enough? Anyway, Daniel and I began to talk." He cleared his throat, remembering the conversations. "Rather, he began to talk and I listened."

"Daniel had a great amount of pride," she murmured as she steeped another batch of tea.

"Yes. Yes, he did."

Sarah had seated herself once again. When she took a chair, he sat across from her. Noticed that her hands were clenched tightly, as if she were striving for control in an uncontrollable situation. "What happened next?" she asked.

"As the days continued to pass ever so slowly, Daniel began to tell me about being Amish. He told me about Ohio, about Holmes County. About this settlement and the people who made it up. He told me about your farm and the way ground was fertile and profitable. He told me about your barn and that kitchen table. He told me about your garden and the abundance of wildlife just beyond you in the woods."

He paused, then plunged ahead and told her the unvarnished truth. "But mostly, Sarah, he talked about you."

And even as he said the words, he ached to take them back. He hated the memories of Daniel speaking about Sarah. Of how he'd bragged about her cooking and sewing and gardening.

And then would act as if those things were of little consequence.

But most of all, John had hated how such a weak, strange, angry man had felt no remorse for discussing his wife in such a public way.

And how he always, always referred to her as part of his property. As if he owned her. As if he was proud of that fact.

All the while never, ever speaking of love.

Ten

· · · · · · · · ·

The Admission

He talked about you.

It was almost miraculous how those four words could bring forth a whole new wave of pain and humiliation.

As Sarah stared at the man she'd thought she knew but was now a stranger, her head began to pound. Suddenly, it was all too much. The harsh memories of her life with Daniel, the grief of realizing she would be alone for the rest of her life, the shock of his return.

And then, most recently, the thin, beautiful ray of hope she'd begun to allow herself to feel. Now, she felt completely devastated.

Staring at Jonathan Scott, realizing how completely he'd fooled her, the pounding in her head grew louder. Soon, it was all she could hear. Her world began to spin as flecks of light and darkness swam before her eyes.

In a vague, hazy way, it occurred to her that she was about to faint. Then she realized that the pressure she'd felt in her lungs wasn't from suppressed emotions.

She'd merely forgotten to breathe. In a rush, she inhaled quickly, before exhaling and taking yet another fortifying breath.

And was finally able to focus again.

Just a few feet away, John stood up, concern etched in his features. "Sarah? Sarah, are you all right?"

When she didn't answer, he stepped forward, obviously ready to come to her aid. "Sarah, what may I get you?"

"Nothing. I mean . . . I am fine."

His expression shuttered as he sat down again. While she got her bearings, he stayed silent. Infinitely patient.

His patience gave her courage to speak. "You said Daniel spoke of me?"

Looking as if his story pained him, John nodded. "You were a source of great pride to him. He, ah, said you were perfect. Perfection." Obviously uncomfortable, he looked as if he were about to say more but pressed his lips together instead.

Somehow, knowing that he, too, found disgrace in Daniel's words made it almost easier to bear. "If I was perfect, it was because he forced perfection from me. It was hard-fought and slowly learned." She closed her eyes, choosing to keep the vivid memories of those lessons to herself. No good would come from John hearing how much pain Daniel's hands had brought to her body. Or the shame his derisive comments had inflicted on her soul.

She couldn't bear for anyone to know just how bad her life with him had been. Especially not this man.

As if he could no longer bear to watch her struggle, John stood up again. Eyeing her with trepidation, he backed up. Truly, there wasn't anywhere for him to go, the room was so small. But still, she could see that he was doing his best to give her a little bit of space. "The picture he painted of you in his words was like no woman I had ever imagined, Sarah. He said you were beautiful. Sweet and devout."

"Daniel had wanted me to be that way." She still wasn't sure if he'd succeeded in tamping out every last bit of spunk inside her. For most of their marriage, it seemed that Daniel hadn't believed he'd succeeded, either. He'd married her because she had been the means to gain a parcel of land, to have one more thing to boast about. But when she'd failed to give him a child, she'd become little more than a reminder of things he wanted but couldn't have.

"All I know was that when I walked onto your land, my only concern was to find the money and leave."

"Money? What money?"

"Daniel told me he'd hidden a large amount on your property. That is the whole reason I came here." He paused, backed up against her kitchen counter. As if giving her a little more space before continuing. "But I would be a liar if I said I came here hoping to never see the woman Daniel had told me so much about. In truth, I yearned to catch a glimpse of you."

"Stop." For reasons she would never know, Daniel had

spun quite a tale to John. She had no desire to hear another minute.

He ignored her. "And that first night, when you caught me in the barn, I drank in the sight of you like a man parched in the desert. And then I knew something else, too."

She glanced up at him, her cheeks warming from his frank words. "And what was that?"

"You were far more than Daniel had described. I was mesmerized."

She yearned to cover her burning face with her hands. To run to the safety of her bedroom. To go anywhere but meet his gaze. His words embarrassed her. Puzzled her.

And, if she were completely honest, his short speech made her desire something she hadn't even realized was vacant from her life until that very moment. "I don't understand why you are telling me about such things," she said. "There is no need."

"There is every need." Pushing back from the counter, he stepped closer. Then, to her further discomfort, he knelt at her feet.

He continued talking, his voice low and rough. Thick with emotion. "I am going to be real honest with you. I didn't care for your husband. I didn't care for his satisfaction in your conduct. I didn't enjoy hearing about the lessons he'd devised to make you bend to his will. Though he was married and a landowner and had a family and the respect of his community, and I had none of that, I knew I would never want to be the man he was."

She felt dizzy. Hated the idea that the memories she'd pushed so far away were threatening to surge forward. Never had she imagined that the things Daniel had forced her to do would be spoken aloud.

But far worse than that was the knowledge that John knew, too. He knew what her life had been like. "Don't speak of it."

But instead of heeding her wishes, he grasped her hands. Linked his fingers through hers and held on tight. "You are more than he ever deserved, Sarah."

Hearing such words was almost irresistible. She fought back the impulse to step closer, to hold him to her. She knew she needed to be stronger. Because though his hands felt almost like a lifeline, one fact remained: He'd lied to her.

In his own way, this man had been just as cruel as Daniel ever was.

With effort, she pulled her fingers from his. "Don't touch me."

"I beg your pardon." Immediately, he released his hold. In a clumsy fashion, he got to his feet and stepped back. "I don't want to hurt you further, Sarah. Though you have no reason to trust me, I promise that I never meant to hurt you. I only came here for Daniel's money."

Her control snapped. "But there is no money. There's nothing! Daniel must have lied to you."

"Daniel told me too much for it all to be lies. I'm sure of that."

"He was good at spinning a tale. He was good at doing whatever it took to make others believe in him."

A line formed between his brows. "I know all about lies and empty promises, Sarah. However, Daniel's story rang true.

He told me all about how he collected funds from the sales of crops to the army. At first they paid him in silver dollars."

"If they did pay him, it wasn't much."

John stepped closer. "He did this for years," he replied, talking over her. "And later, when all landowners were required to give everything over to the Union, he saved and scrimped and hoarded his pennies."

She shook her head.

"Sarah, he boasted about it continuously."

"But we had nothing. We went hungry."

"Before he left, he hid it all in or near your barn."

"That canna be true."

"He swore it to be true."

"I still don't understand why you are here."

He averted his eyes, as if he was too embarrassed to confess. "I spent the last couple of months in a series of hospital encampments, struggling for my life. Struggling to overcome the pain." His voice lowered to a mere whisper. "Struggling to resign myself to looking like this. To losing most of the feeling in my cheek, on the left side of my body. Of being scarred. Damaged. Ruined."

"You are not ruined, John," she blurted, unable to help herself. After all, she knew what it felt like to be damaged.

He ignored her. "When I was discharged, I walked out of the base realizing that I had nothing. No money, no family. I was disfigured and in pain. All I had was a uniform marked with lieutenant's bars—but I wasn't even fit to serve. Sarah, I had nothing."

Sarah tried to imagine such a thing but she couldn't.

Couldn't imagine any friend of his not offering him shelter during his time of need. After all, he'd already lost so much fighting for his country.

"I am sorry for that."

He shook his head. "Don't pity me. I don't know why I'm telling you this, except that I yearn for you to understand what led me here." He sat down in the chair across from her. "I felt adrift and alone. I needed something to believe in, something to give me hope. And as sad and terrible as it sounds, the only thing I had was the idea of finding Daniel's money. Soon, it seemed it was all I thought about."

"So you came here to live his life?"

"Not at all. It was as I told you. I came here to take your money. To steal from you." He looked down at his feet, as if he couldn't bear to meet her eyes. "I came here to take what was rightfully yours. I was going to take it and go out West. Thinking that maybe somewhere in Texas or the Oklahoma Territory, they would have me. But then?"

"But then I found you."

"You did. On only my third night." He shook his head in dismay. Looking rueful. "See, I made a terrible mistake, Sarah. I never asked enough questions. When the explosion hit our encampment and your husband died and I became like . . . like this, I only had the barest information about the money. And a whole lot of information about you and his Amish way of life."

She was starting to understand. "You remembered it all because he had so much . . ."

"Yes. Because he had so much and I had nothing."

"I couldn't believe it when I saw you, that first night." She swallowed. "I . . . I did believe you were my husband."

"Men had told Daniel and me that we looked eerily alike. Our eyes were almost the same color, our builds much the same. You may not ever believe me, but I promise you this, I never, ever thought that you would find me. I never intended to move in here. But when you called me Daniel and then fainted, I knew I couldn't simply leave you. Not when I felt like I knew you."

"But when I woke up?"

"I didn't think. I acted like a fool. At first it was mere preservation. I knew if I told you the truth I would have to leave and I would have nothing. And I didn't want 'nothing' any longer. So I told myself I'd pretend to be your husband for just a while."

"Until you found the money," she murmured.

"Yes. But I justified it, too." Shaking his head slightly, he said, "I knew how he treated you. I knew how he'd thought of you. It pained me. I saw the distrust in your eyes. I saw fear and hurt and exhaustion etched in your beautiful face and I wanted to erase it. And so I made a vow to myself. I decided to do what I could to try to make up his treatment of you. I thought I would help you. Treat you kindly. Help you get back on your feet. Then I would leave, and you would be at least a little better off than before."

"How am I better off?" she asked. "All this time, I've been so confused. I felt hurt. I didn't understand how the war could have changed you so much. Not just your looks, but your whole personality.

"John, I don't think you have any idea about how I've felt. When Daniel left, I didn't miss him, I felt *relief*. And then, hearing that he'd died—all while I'd been secretly glad he was gone? The guilt I felt . . . well, it was extraordinary."

When he tried to interrupt, she held up a hand. She wasn't sure why she needed to share so much but she did. For some reason, divulging her secrets felt cleansing.

But she wasn't done.

"When I first saw you? Thinking you were Daniel, back from the dead? I felt like the Lord was punishing me. But then, as we spent more time together, I began to thank the Lord for bringing you back." She shook her head. "So, your plot and schemes were not so good after all, Jonathan Scott. See, instead of making my life better, you have made it so much worse."

At his harsh intake of breath, she forced herself to look directly in his eyes. "See, when I began to trust you, I felt that God had granted me redemption. He'd forgiven me for not mourning Daniel like I should have. He'd given me a second chance to be a better person."

"Being relieved your husband wasn't hurting you is not wrong, Sarah. Neither is being grateful for being treated kindly. You have done nothing wrong."

"I did everything wrong. I've become a person I don't recognize." She left it at that, and hoped he wouldn't ask what she meant. She couldn't bear to admit just how deep her feelings ran for him. She couldn't bear to admit that she'd been sure she was falling in love with him.

The pain in his eyes showed that he wasn't having an

easier time with their conversation. "Sarah, I don't know how to leave you without causing you more problems."

Suddenly, she was exhausted. She turned to go to sleep. "I suppose we'll solve that problem *verra* soon. But for now? For now I am going to sleep."

"You don't want me to leave right now?"

"The room? *Jah*."

"The house? The farm?"

"In the middle of the night?" She shook her head. "We have too much to discuss. Things better left for the new day."

"Oh. Yes. Yes, of course. Because everything is sure to look different in a few hours."

She turned away, not wanting him to see that she completely agreed with his derisive comment. It was going to take far more than a new day to finish their discussion. To figure out what to do next.

It was going to take even longer to wrap her mind around the fact that not only had John been lying to her about pretty much everything . . . but that she had eagerly believed his lies. She'd been so ready to have the life she'd fantasized about. A life with someone who treated her with respect and dignity.

And because of that, she'd accepted his kindness. Dared to believe his compliments.

But worst of all, she'd allowed herself to hope. To be happy.

Now? Now, she had nothing, all over again.

Eleven

· · · · · · · · · ·

The Partnership

JOHN HAD ALREADY been up a full hour by the time the sun broke over the horizon. After milking the cow, he'd entered the still-dark kitchen, brewed a pot of coffee, and then nursed cup after cup of the strong brew, staring at Sarah's closed bedroom door in the morning's silence.

As he did, he wondered if she'd arisen. Wondered if she had considered forgiving him.

And then he found himself contemplating why he hadn't already left.

He hadn't been able to sleep much the night before. Now that his dark secret had been broken, he was too restless with nervous energy. He was guilt-ridden, too. Never would he forget the way her face had looked when she'd realized the full extent of his lies.

What he had done had been unforgivable. If she never wanted to see him again, he wouldn't blame her one bit. But still he stayed.

He wanted to believe that he stayed out of concern for Sarah. But inside, he knew that wasn't the case.

No, he was merely staying for himself. He didn't want to leave his life with her. It had become too dear to him.

Sarah made an appearance when he was pouring his fifth cup of coffee. She looked as she always did, her clothing neat, her hair carefully twisted and fastened under her *kapp*. Only her red eyes hinted at their tumultuous night—and the strain he'd put her through.

He ached to ease her. "Sit down, Sarah. I'll get you some of your coffee and milk."

A mixture of emotions passed through her face before she replied. "John, I'll have you know that I drink *kaffi* in the morning. Not *kaffi* and milk."

He couldn't believe that she was joking with him. "You drink warm milk with a splash of coffee. And then you add enough sugar to make one's teeth fairly sing."

She pretended to look mildly affronted. "Surely I don't add that much."

"You add enough. Surely a heaping teaspoon." He grinned as he prepared her coffee just the way she liked it and then handed it to her with a small bow.

"It is hardly worth mentioning." She took the mug and sipped. Closed her eyes in obvious pleasure, then sipped again.

"Maybe not. Or maybe so," he quipped, taking care to

keep his voice easy and light. Gentle on her frayed nerves. "Maybe it's because I've been surrounded by so many men in my life, but I've never seen anything like the sweet, creamy beverage you call coffee. Does it taste okay?"

"It is *wunderbaar.*"

She looked so pleased with something so small, John felt his heart twist a bit again. He was finding it hard to hide his burgeoning feelings for her.

"I saw a beehive outside. If you want, I'll try and coax some honey from those bees."

Alarm filled her blue eyes. "*Nee!* You might get stung!"

Whether it was masculine pride, or the fact that he could obviously handle something as slight as a bee sting, he chuckled. "I promise, I'll gladly accept a bee's sting as a trade for your honey." But when he noticed her eyes had teared up, he stopped his blustering and crouched in front of her. "What's really wrong?"

"I'm afraid of bees. Please don't go near that hive."

He yearned to reach out and cradle her face in his hands. To press his lips against her cheeks to stop the flow of tears.

"I won't," he promised.

"*Danke.* I . . . I know it's silly."

"It's not silly if it's important to you."

After a pause, she said quietly, "Daniel thought my fear was unfounded. He didn't understand why I wanted to purchase sugar when we had so much honey on the property."

"If it makes you happy, you should have it."

Wonder filled her gaze. "You mean that, don't you?"

He nodded and, realizing he was about to stroke her face,

stood up. "It seems like a little enough thing. I would venture to say that every man should be so lucky to have a woman so easy to please. Shoot. I'd give you a cupful of sugar with each cup of coffee if it would make you smile." Of course, the moment he said those words he ached to take them back. He had no business speaking to her in such a fashion. He was being too personal—and talking as if they were even going to have a future one day.

Luckily, she didn't seem to take offense. Instead, she gazed at him thoughtfully.

He felt another odd tug around his heart. He wondered how she'd react to him hugging her. Kissing her. But of course the moment the thought crossed his mind, he pushed it away, feeling ashamed of himself. He should be trying hard to ease her worries, not daydreaming about holding her in his arms.

He cleared his throat and forced himself to return to their conversation from the night before. "Sarah, we should probably discuss last night."

"*Jah.* We should."

"Have you changed your mind about me leaving this morning?"

She paused. "*Nee.*" She set her now-empty coffee cup on the table. "Believe it or not, your indifference to that sugar was one of the first things that made me wonder if you were truly Daniel," she murmured. "I couldn't understand why you never cared."

He ached to tell her that he'd spoken far too lightly of Daniel Ropp the night before. In truth, her husband had been the worst sort of man. He ached to tell her that he couldn't imagine any other man caring so much about something so little.

But he was the last person to throw stones.

"Well, it turns out that you were exactly right to be suspicious, Sarah. In fact, you could spend all day listing ways that I've deceived you," he admitted. "I'd rather you didn't do that."

"And why is that?"

He thought quickly and realized that he was holding on to the hope that she wouldn't kick him out. He didn't want to go back to merely subsisting. He didn't want to leave and once again fend for everything, from food to shelter to even the basic dignity he desired. He didn't want to be looked at as a source of both pity and derision. As if he should have either survived the war with his whole self intact . . . or had the dignity to die.

But most of all, he didn't want to leave her.

"Because there's nothing I can do about the past," he finally said. "What's done is done."

"I agree. I don't know if it's possible, but I would enjoy brushing the past away. But is it really that easy?"

"I hope so. I'd like for it to be."

She still looked uncomfortable. "I am not altogether sure what we should do. Last night, all I wanted was for you to leave the farm. But this morning when I woke up, I wasn't sure if that was the right thing to do, either."

"What do you think changed your mind?"

"You." She shrugged. "And me, too, perhaps." Looking restless, she stood up and walked her cup to the container of soapy water. "When I first married Daniel, I had stars in my eyes. I had a young girl's foolish dreams about what married life was like." Lowering her gaze, she said, "I soon realized, however, that reality was nothing like that. I tried to talk to my parents about my pain, but my mother told me that I shouldn't speak of such things."

"Where are they now?"

She swallowed. "Gone. Scarlet fever ran through our community shortly after Daniel and I wed. Many in our community passed on into heaven then."

She'd been so alone for so long, John could hardly believe it. Just like him, she'd been surrounded by people, but essentially subsisting alone.

Taking a fortifying breath, John tried to soothe her, to at least let her know that her feelings were valid. That she'd been right to think so much of what happened in her marriage had been so terribly wrong.

"Daniel's cruelty was never your fault, Sarah. I don't know what all he made you do, or every terrible thing he subjected you to, but I know in my heart that the problem was his."

"You sound so sure."

"You forget; I spent many an hour by his side. I heard how he talked of marriage and his wife. And now I know you, too. He was wrong. He was wrong about so much."

She rubbed her temple. "Your words are like nothing I've ever heard before. They make me confused."

"I do apologize."

"John, what I mean to say is that now I am not all that certain about what is right and what is wrong. It was wrong for you to arrive here wrapped in lies. And perhaps it is wrong for me not to cast you out. But I am also starting to wonder if, perhaps, the Lord brought us together for some reason that we can only dare to guess at now."

John knew how she was feeling. More than once he'd wondered how he'd ended up next to an Amish man in a trench in Pennsylvania—and why that man had felt the need to tell him all his secrets.

He wasn't ready to share that, though. At this moment, he felt like it was Sarah's choice. She needed to be in control, not him. "What would you like to do?" he asked softly.

She dipped the cup into water, swirling it gently with her hand. "Wait," she said after a moment. "I'd like to wait a bit. Wait until the shock of it all has faded. I feel like we need to make the right decisions now. But I am not sure what they are."

Everything she said was true. He knew, no matter what, he would abide by her decision—even if she told him to pack up his gunnysack and leave within the hour.

But that said, he also knew it was time for him to speak his mind. He sat down next to her. "Sarah, I've been up most of the night thinking about this. Thinking about you and me."

She raised her brows. "And the money jar?"

"Yes." He couldn't lie about that. "Sarah, of course that money is yours. Yours and Daniel's. Since he isn't here to retrieve it, why don't I help you find it? I'd be honored to know that I helped you be a little better off."

"If it's there . . ."

"It's there. I'm sure of it."

"And after you give it to me? Then what would you do?"

He knew what he'd want to do. He would want to stay with her for as long as she'd have him. That, however, was certainly a silly wish. "Whatever you wanted."

She blinked. "You continue to surprise me."

"I imagine that you will always think the worst of me. It is no less than I deserve. Sarah, there are no amends I can make for the things I have done. My only excuse is that my actions were made by a desperate man. One who'd learned to beg, borrow, and steal to survive."

After drying her mug with a rag, she said, "I've been thinking about that jar, too. It symbolizes a great many things, John. So many evil things, things that make me uncomfortable. Right now, I'm not sure that I even want to find it."

"Of course you do," he replied before she could voice another doubt. "Sarah, I know you know far more about honesty and integrity than I ever could. It's admirable, and I hold you in esteem for that. But, at the end of the day, not everything in life can be gotten with a good character. Sometimes only money will do. And I promise, one day you are going to need that money."

"I imagine I will. But I fear it will always feel like a hindrance instead of a gift. He purposely hid it from me. All this time. Did he even care for me, do you suppose?"

John knew that answer. Daniel Ropp had cared about only one person, and that was himself. He'd been a selfish soldier, a vindictive, arrogant friend, and a far worse husband.

Furthermore, Daniel had been blessed with a sweet and

lovely wife who'd remained true to him even after his death. She'd been almost shunned by those in her community who firmly believed that her husband had strayed from everything their faith held dear.

Of course, none of what Daniel had done excused John's own transgressions. He'd taken advantage of the situation and had used it for his own selfish purposes.

His only consolation had been that he'd known what he'd had, and that was nothing. He'd had no home, no sweetheart, no family waiting for him or looking out for him.

"John, tell me the truth." Her eyes were filled with pain; her voice was thick, husky.

And he knew in that instant that he couldn't bear to tell her another lie. "No," he finally said. "I don't think Daniel cared for you at all."

She closed her eyes and swallowed. It was easy to see that she was blinking back tears. "*Danke* for telling me the truth."

"It was true that Daniel didn't love you. But he should have," he said quickly, surprised to hear that his voice sounded just as emotional as hers did. "Daniel was a lucky man, a blessed man, to have a woman like you. It is to his shame that he treated you so dishonorably. Any other man would have treated you far better."

"Maybe. Maybe not."

"Sarah, even people who do not love each other do not treat one another the way he treated you. It was wrong. Please believe me."

"I didn't love him. Part of me feared him. But I have to admit that I did wish things were different."

"That seems only natural. Marriage is for life. Most people do ache for a partner in life."

"But you do not."

"I told you my story last night. I've never had the luxury to feel like I could go courting or take on a wife. I had nothing to offer anyone."

"If you stay here until we find the money jar and then leave, you will still have nothing."

"No, I will. I'll finally have something to be proud of."

"Even more than your war record?"

He thought about that. Thought about how proud he'd been when he'd made the jump from a mere enlisted foot soldier to an officer. Until this moment, that had been the highlight of his life. "Even more than that."

She stared at him hard, then nodded. "So for now we will look for the money jar together. After that? We'll cross that bridge when we come to it."

"And if people stop by to see you? To see us? What do you want to tell them?"

"And if anyone stops by we will let them believe that you are my husband, Daniel. For now, that seems to be the best way to go."

Her words made him so happy. For the first time in days he felt as if he was at peace. "All right, Sarah. If that is your wish."

"It is. Now step aside so I can make us some breakfast," she said briskly. "If you're going to hunt for that jar in the light of day, you're going to need to eat."

With a smile, he stepped to the side, out of her way. And grinned to himself when she smiled right back.

Twelve

· · · · · · · · · ·

The Confrontation

DANIEL ROPP HAD been back a full month.

Zeke knew in his heart that pure jealousy, mixed with an unhealthy dose of needless curiosity, propelled him to decide to visit the Ropps' farm. And though he'd told his sister Ana that he would stay far away from Sarah, he'd slowly had come to terms with the fact that he could no longer keep his promise. He wasn't proud of himself.

But there was something wrong with Sarah's relationship with her husband. And there was something definitely different about Daniel. Other people in the community had noticed it, too, though no one had come right out and blatantly said so. But there had been numerous discussions, with all of them wondering why he didn't seem to remember them much. About how tentative he seemed around Sarah, whereas before Daniel had always been foolishly arrogant.

Even his way of speaking sounded foreign and odd. It was as if he had to carefully weigh every word that he spoke. Almost as if English had been his first language instead of Pennsylvania Dutch.

All that together, combined with the fact that his features weren't quite how they should be—burn or no burn—equaled a great many inconsistencies. Surely so many that they couldn't be denied. The more he thought about all of Daniel's discrepancies, the more Zeke started to worry. He began to imagine all sorts of fantastical things and that the man had been lying to Sarah while she was too good of a person to ever suspect such a thing.

In his worst moments, Zeke had begun to fear that Sarah was in grave danger. That she was trapped on the property with a madman, begging silently for help.

He feared the very privacy they all were trying to give her was to her detriment.

He didn't even dare ask himself what he thought he could do if that was the case. Would he risk going against the church's policies to fend off an evil man if Sarah needed help?

When he reached the property, his curiosity was further piqued. The sun was shining, as it was almost mid-morning. Most women would have clothes hanging on the line by now. Instead, the house looked dark and quiet.

He stood, flummoxed, until he heard voices floating out from the barn's open doors.

Glad he had decided to walk to the farm instead of riding his horse, Zeke stopped and listened. Tried to gauge who was inside. If Sarah was alone, he would go right in.

But then, all at once, he heard a deep voice murmur something . . . and it was followed by Sarah chuckling.

That ringing, beautiful sound brought him up short. When had he last heard her sound so joyful?

To his dismay, he couldn't remember a time. Not since she was a child, at least.

There was low conversation again, followed by Sarah's melodic reply. Drawn to the noise, Zeke walked to the open doorway before he could stop himself. Or, at the very least, formulate an explanation about why he had arrived.

The sight he discovered fairly took his breath away. Daniel was sitting atop an old table, tapping the barn's wall behind him. Sarah was perched on a chair nearby. And, to Zeke's further dismay, it looked as if she were directing her husband.

She had just leaned forward, telling Daniel to tap harder on one of the cracked boards, when she spied him.

Abruptly, she got to her feet and sobered. "Zeke! My goodness, you gave me a start! Were you standing here long?"

"Not too long."

"Did you go to the *haus* already?"

"*Nee.* I heard voices in here." Sarah's cheeks pinkened at his words, and Zeke imagined she was mighty embarrassed. He'd never heard of a woman sitting on a chair in the barn in the middle of the day. It had been most odd behavior.

Daniel put down the tool he'd been holding, staring all the while at Zeke in a cool, assessing way. It made Zeke a bit uncomfortable. And made him realize that he was surely overstepping his bounds. It was obvious that Daniel did not care for another man passing judgment on him—or his wife.

And it was such a reaction that Daniel would have that Zeke wondered, for the very first time, if he had been wrong.

He stood there, eyeing them, as Daniel hopped off the table he was sitting on. "Zeke Graber, *jah*?"

"*Jah*."

"How may I be of service to you?"

Instantly, Zeke relaxed. There was yet another odd phrase—a phrase no Amish man would offer. After pulling off his hat, he held it between his hands. "I, ah, wanted to stop by. To check on things, you know. To make sure everyone was all right."

Daniel's eyes narrowed. "Why would you have such worries?"

"I, uh, thought that you might not be fully recovered from your wounds." Zeke let his statement drift between them, then, at last, said what was on his mind. "And I was concerned about Sarah's welfare."

Sarah's eyes widened. "Me?"

Daniel motioned for her to keep quiet and for her stay where she was. Just as if Sarah had something to fear from Zeke! The idea was so wrong, was so mistaken, it made Zeke's temper flare.

"I came here to speak to both of you. I would appreciate it if you would let her speak. After all, Sarah has nothing to fear from me."

Daniel crossed his arms over his chest. "Maybe not. Maybe I am the one who should be afraid." He stepped a little closer, stopping right in front of Zeke so that Zeke had no option but to stare at the muscles lying just underneath the scars on Daniel's arms, at the jagged skin on his face. At the eye that didn't quite focus.

And his demeanor was so stoic, so calm, it made Zeke feel ashamed.

At last, Daniel spoke. "As you can see, I don't look real pretty, but I work all right. I can also see to the needs of my *frau*. *Danke* for your concern, but it is unwarranted. However, maybe you can tell me why you are you were concerned about my wife?"

If they were talking about anyone else, Zeke would have apologized. He was no fool. He knew it wasn't right to be so concerned about another man's wife.

But this was Sarah, and this man still seemed like a stranger, and their history together had been bad. "You know why. She is a gentle soul. And you—" He bit off the rest of his words, not quite willing to utter everything he was thinking.

"And me?" One eyebrow lifted.

Zeke sighed. "And you are not."

"And so therefore you came over out of the goodness of your heart." Daniel's voice was tinged with sarcasm.

It almost embarrassed him.

"Oh, Zeke," Sarah said.

"It's all right, Sarah. Don't fret." Then, Daniel's voice hardened as he turned to face Zeke. "For the record, I think you are exactly right. I am absolutely a man who has now seen too much. There is little gentle about me. There never has been. But that doesn't mean my wife has anything to fear. I must tell you that I am not altogether pleased to be told this to my face, however."

"There are many in the community who do not trust you."

"Then I will have to gain their trust," Daniel said as he crossed his arms in front of his chest.

Suddenly, he looked much bigger. Far more formidable. Everything in Zeke's body told him to step back, to leave. But he knew if he did, he would always regret it.

Gathering his courage, he said, "You won't be able to gain anyone's trust. In time, we will all see you for what you are."

"What is that?" Daniel asked.

"Daniel, Zeke, please, let us not fight," Sarah interrupted. "Let us not ruin the day. After all, it is so rare that we have company."

"Is it? Sarah said you visited her while I was gone."

"Of course I did. She needed some help now and then."

"I am grateful for your concern. Sarah was blessed to have a *friend* like you. However, as you can see, everything is fine now. I hope you will be relieved about that, and have no further cause for concern."

Zeke knew he should take Daniel's words as a stern warning and leave. But he also realized that once he left he would have lost his opportunity to check on Sarah. "What are you doing in here? Why were you tapping the walls?"

Daniel shrugged. "Merely making repairs."

Zeke craned his head around Daniel, attempting to get a better view of the walls. "What sort of repairs? I've looked at the walls a time or two. They looked fine to me."

"They are rotting."

"But why do you have so many other things out?" Even as he said the words, Zeke knew he'd gone too far. No man would put up with such intrusive questions—and no man should have to.

Daniel's eyes narrowed. "I fear I am losing patience. Why are you concerned? Why are you coming over uninvited and asking questions about our home and farm? Sarah is no longer alone. There is no longer a reason for you to stop over. Unannounced."

Sarah gripped the edge of her apron. "Zeke, we are going to have dinner soon. Please, stay and enjoy the meal with us."

"Yes, join us," Daniel echoed. "I would enjoy hearing the answers to my questions. And why you feel like you can cast stones."

Daniel's eyes looked so cool, so accusing, that Zeke took a step back. And realized that he had to retreat emotionally as well. "*Danke*, but I fear I must be going. I only wanted to stop by."

"And now you have," Daniel murmured.

Though he felt utterly miserable, Zeke forced himself to look directly at Sarah. "I hope I my visit will not cause you any ill feelings. I promise, I came here with the best of intentions."

Her gaze was soft. "I know that, Zeke." Then, to Zeke's amazement, Sarah stepped to her husband's side. "But I am afraid that it would be best if you didn't come over again."

He felt as if his heart was breaking all over again. Before he could blame circumstances and timing for his loss, but now it was completely evident that his love for her was neither appreciated nor accepted.

This time, she had rejected him.

And as he began his long walk home, Zeke knew that he would not forget this pain anytime soon.

And neither would he forget his anger toward Daniel. The man didn't deserve her and had now made things worse.

This moment would not be forgotten.

Thirteen

· · · · · · · · ·

The Choice

AFTER THREE DAYS of practically taking the barn apart inch by inch, Sarah was feeling frustrated. And stiff and sore. And more than a little confused. Sometime between deciding that she was going to need to let John stay in order to locate the hidden money and this very moment, her feelings for the mysterious man had begun to change.

And, she realized, she'd begun to change, too.

After living in a state of numbness for the last couple of years, she had slowly begun to feel hopeful. Instead of resigning herself to basically living in solitude for years and years, she'd begun to look forward to spending time with John.

The fact that he was English, pretending to be her husband, and would eventually leave was—for the moment, at least—inconsequential. Instead, she was finding it hard to resist the one person who seemed to genuinely care about her.

And with whom she was starting to feel a sense of peace.

As she scanned the debris littering the ground around their feet with an ill-concealed grimace, she gave in to weakness. "John, may we take a break today? All I can think about is how much time this is going to take to put it all back together."

With an exhale, he put down the crowbar he'd been using to lift some of the floorboards and turned to her. "I suppose we could. We have been working hard."

"We've been working terribly hard."

His eyes lit with amusement, telling her without words that he'd worked far harder for far longer many a time. "What would you like to do?"

"Could we . . . could we simply go for a walk?"

"Of course we could. I'd like that."

Pleased, and slightly embarrassed to be so pleased with so little, Sarah climbed to her feet. "I could pack us a picnic, even."

He rubbed his jaw. "A picnic, hmm?"

"Or not."

"*Nee*, truly going on a picnic sounds wonderful." He rubbed his jaw again. It was clean-shaven. He'd tried to grow the beard that all married Amish men had but the scars on his face had prevented it from coming in evenly. "I simply don't believe I've ever gone on one before."

"Not even when you were a child?"

"Especially not when I was a child." Obviously seeing that

she was preparing to ask more about that, he pulled off his work gloves. "How about you pack us a lunch while I clean up?"

"I'll be happy to do that. I promise, it won't take long."

"Take as long as you need. I am suddenly finding myself eager to get out of this barn."

She practically scampered to the house like a child, she was so excited. And, to her amusement, she found herself humming as she put together a stack of bread and butter sandwiches, spicy pickle spears, and the remainder of the fried rabbit she'd cooked the night before. After wrapping it all in a pair of bandannas, she gathered a quilt, two mason jars full of lemonade, and a good-sized metal pail. She was just arranging the food-filled bandannas and the mason jars in the pail when John came to the door.

"Do you need any help?"

"I might need your help carrying everything."

He chuckled. "Besides that, Sarah. Of course I wasn't going to make you carry anything."

She ducked her head, not wanting him to see her expression. John did that a lot, she was realizing. He teased her gently, encouraged her in his quiet way to relax a little bit more each day. Relaxing around him was still a struggle. Old habits of Daniel finding fault with her were deeply embedded.

To her surprise, however, she was slowly forgetting to guard her words. It gave her both a newfound freedom and a curious sense of exhilaration.

"Are you ready now?"

"I think so."

"Well, come on then. Our day of playing hooky is upon us."

She followed him out the door, choosing to carry the quilt while he held the tin pail. "I fear I don't know what that phrase means."

"It means that we're taking some time off, but we're being sneaky about it." He gave her a little bow, looking gallant and much like the officer he had been. "After you, my dear."

She ached to say something spunky in return but words failed her. So instead, she pointed to a clear path in the thicket of trees. "There's a path there that leads to a creek. Have you seen it yet?"

"No. But I would like to. Lead the way and I'll follow."

She felt herself blush because of the way his words sounded, though she was sure he'd meant nothing romantic by them.

But her reaction made her even more determined to put their relationship—or lack of it—into perspective. What she was imagining happening was probably nothing more than a reaction to simple kindness.

For years now she'd witnessed her friends' marriages. When she'd dared to dwell on them, she'd realized that the husbands treated their wives far differently than Daniel had treated her. Though they were still most definitely the head of the household, they did not eye their women with disdain or seek to embarrass them in front of others in the community.

Instead, a quiet fondness rested between them, illustrated in small words and tender gestures.

It seemed that was what John was doing. The experience was new and strange, and she felt awkward as she attempted to match his movements and comments.

And hopelessly out of her element.

"I, ah, don't usually walk too fast," she warned.

"I don't want to walk fast. If we're going to enjoy our day, then I want to take our time."

She couldn't think of any other warnings or responses to that, so off they started, at first with her walking in the lead, then eventually walking side by side as the winding, narrow path allowed. Their pace was anything but brisk. In fact, it bordered on meandering. Strolling.

Every few feet one of them would spy something worth pointing out, even if it wasn't anything very much at all. John spied a snake curled up under a bush. Sleeping. She liked looking for cardinals and orioles.

Soon, her words eased, matching her even steps. She stopped stumbling over words and slid into his easy conversation. Soon, she was responding to all his comments, about anything and everything. She was discovering that not only was her pretend husband a wealth of information, he was also curious by nature. He asked question after question about being Amish and her feelings regarding it.

That in itself was a wondrous thing. Until John, she'd had little to no contact with the English. Ever. The men in their community dealt with outsiders. She'd gotten used to thinking of the Englischers as coarse and arrogant men. Dangerous, too.

But John was showing her that she'd made a grievous error in clumping all men who weren't Amish into one group.

At last they arrived on the banks of the creek.

"What's the name of this body of water?"

"It's Sugar Creek." She smiled slightly, thinking he was the first person she'd met who hadn't known the name of one of their county's biggest landmarks.

Kneeling down, he reached into the bubbling creek and let his fingers flutter in the water. The look that crossed over his features was one of pure bliss. She wondered if the cool water soothed his scarred skin.

"Do you come here often?" he asked, interrupting her thoughts. "I mean, when you can?"

After a moment's hesitation, Sarah knelt next to him on the creek bed. "Not so much. I mean, not so much anymore. I used to when I was a young girl."

"When you were a young girl, hmm?" One side of his lips turned up. "I'm trying to imagine you as anything other than prim and proper. Was that what you were like?"

"Maybe. I've always been rather quiet." For a moment, she ached to tell him more, to add something, but she decided against it. No man wanted to hear a woman continually chatter about herself.

After pulling his hand out of the cool creek, he shook it a few times, then stretched his legs out in front of him so that his whole scarred side faced the creek, and leaned back on his hands. "Surely you can do better than that, Sarah. What is there to be afraid of? Before you know it, I'll be gone and never have a chance to tell your secrets."

His quip hit her hard. It hurt to even imagine what her life was going to be like after he was gone. But this was a time for them to relax, not dwell on their problems. "I'm definitely not sharing my secrets with you," she teased, tilting her chin up for good measure.

"Is it because you don't have any? Or you don't trust me enough?"

"I guess it's a bit of both." She reached into the pail, pulled out the jars of lemonade, and handed him one. After taking a fortifying sip, she said, "If I share something with you, will you share with me, too?"

"Yes." But she noticed that he didn't look all that eager to divulge something too personal, either.

"All right. I, um, used to catch frogs here."

"That's your big secret?"

Feeling a little embarrassed, she looked at him out of the corner of her eye. "*Jah*. Why? What's wrong with that?"

"Nothing . . . except that it's not personal."

"I suppose it is not." She leaned back on her elbows, only noticing after she was settled that she mirrored his position.

He sighed. "I suppose I'm going to have to help you out. Where did you receive your first kiss?"

"That is nothing we should discuss, Jonathan Scott."

To her dismay—and yet, to her amusement, too—he let out a bark of laughter. "You sound like a mother, using my first and last name like that. I have now been firmly chastised."

"*Das gut*. Because I will not talk about kisses." Especially since she didn't have too many to share. Daniel had been the one and only man she had ever kissed. And his kisses had been neither frequent nor particularly pleasant.

"Fine. Tell me a regret."

The plea hit her hard, almost taking the breath out of her. "I doubt you want to hear any of those," she hedged.

"I wouldn't have asked if I didn't want to hear. Come on, Sarah, isn't there one that you can share?"

She didn't like this game of his. She didn't like being forced to think about things that she'd pushed aside for years, pretending they didn't matter so that she wouldn't feel any pain. "I regret that I never had any *kinner*. Any children."

His teasing expression sobered. "Ah. I imagine so. I think you would be a wonderful mother."

She inclined her head. Her tongue felt too thick to respond. "Is it your turn now?"

"Yes. If you want it to be."

"Do your scars hurt all the time?"

This time he was the one who looked terribly uncomfortable. "No."

"That is your answer?"

He looked away from her, as if he couldn't bear to be exposed in so many ways. "Do you mind me asking why you care?"

She cared because she hated to think of him in constant pain. And she was beginning to care about him very much. "I noticed the look on your face when you dipped your fingers in the creek."

"The cold water feels good. He held out his right arm in front of him, looking at it like it belonged to another person, as if he wasn't quite sure how it had come to be on his body. "The scars, they make my skin feel tight. Like there's not enough skin to cover. It's not as much painful as uncomfortable. The doctors said that will ease in time."

"I hope that is the case."

"Me too." He paused, then added, "I don't like talking about how I look."

"It's nothing to be ashamed of."

"I'm not ashamed, but I'm not all that used to it. Not to sound too prideful, but I used to be a handsome man. When I was younger, I'd catch the girls sneaking glances at me. I was used to that. I'm ashamed to admit that at times I have difficulty realizing I'm now a person women turn away from. I hate to see myself in the mirror."

She could only imagine what that must be like. Just as quickly, she amended her thoughts. She had no earthly idea what his trials had been like. Feeling somewhat at a loss, she said the first thing on her mind. "Luckily, we Amish don't believe in looking glasses."

He turned his head and stared at her strangely, then he grinned. "There is that."

"Are you ready to eat?"

"I am. I'm anxious to snack on our picnic lunch then lie about and be lazy. What about you?"

"I feel the same way." She was anxious to run her hands in the cool water, too. Anxious to feel even a little bit of his bliss.

Fourteen

....

The Remembrance

THE NEXT MORNING, John found himself back near the barn. He wasn't sure if their outing the day before had rejuvenated his spirit or brought him even more sorrow . He was inclined to think of the latter.

All his life he'd ached to belong. And now, in a strange, unnatural way, he felt that he did belong to Sarah. As he walked around the outside perimeter of the barn early that morning, he tried to imagine what he was going to feel when he discovered the money and gave it to her.

Relief, probably. And maybe a sense of completion. Something to hold tight in his soul whenever he realized that he was basically just a worthless ex-soldier. At least once in his life, he'd tried to do something worthwhile.

Remembering yet again all his conversations with Daniel,

he eyed the rough planks on the outside of the barn. Wondering again why he was having such a difficult time finding something that had to look so obvious.

As he ran his hand along the wood, he let his mind drift. He stopped attempting to recall every conversation in its entirety. Instead, he allowed himself to recall mere phrases. Parts of conversations.

When he felt a pinch, he lifted his hand and noticed a sizable splinter had wedged itself along one of his knuckles. Carefully, he pulled it out, somewhat taken aback that his scarred hand could feel anything at all.

And then he recalled the last time he'd pulled out such a splinter. He'd been complaining to Daniel about the rotten wood they were burning . . . complaining that it was infested with vermin. Daniel had merely laughed and called him a weakling. "Never thought I'd see the day when our lieutenant let a few hornets and splinters get the best of him."

"They've hardly gotten the best of me. I just don't have a need to get scratched and stung. We've got enough problems with the Johnny Rebs."

Daniel had remained unimpressed. "You're acting as childish as my wife."

"And why is that?" he'd asked, somewhat bored. If there was anything Daniel had liked to do, it was talk. And talk he did, mostly about how smart he was . . . and how good he was at ordering his wife about. The more John listened, the less he'd wanted to hear. Actually, the longer he'd been in Daniel's company, the more he'd ached to be done with him. There was so much in the man that John had found fault with.

While it was true that they both had brown hair and eyes, and that they were much of the same height and build, those were their only similarities. Though Daniel might have had money to save and was a landowner, at least John hadn't spent the last several years being mean to a woman.

"You're acting like my wife because she's scared to death of bees." Daniel's voice had been almost gleeful. "She got stung real bad by an angry swarm when she was a little girl. The midwife even had to come over and help her *mamm* pull out stingers. She told me once it was her worst and earliest memory. Anyway, that old oak has a real good-sized hive in it. When we first got married, Sarah asked me to get rid of it, but I wasn't having any of her complaining. I told her that we were going to keep it and that was final. And that, you see, is why I ended up hiding my money near that tree. Why, I could have tied banknotes to the branches and she wouldn't have gone near them!"

John had been so sickened by Daniel's bragging, knowing that he'd willingly kept something nearby because it scared his wife, that he'd stood up and moved away from him.

And then, mere moments later, the sparks had flown and the fire had come. The whole conversation had been forgotten.

Until right this minute.

Feeling a strange combination of both dread and anticipation, John walked around the barn again. But this time, instead of merely looking at the barn's planks, he scanned the trees that surrounded it.

After another two or three minutes, John located the beehive. It wasn't real big but it was definitely populated with enough buzzing residents to give most anyone pause.

He imagined Sarah would have been terrified, given her aversion to honey and honeybees.

Then he began to pat the wall. Slowly, looking for loose boards, uneven cuts. Holes that didn't look quite right.

And then, there, a mere foot above the ground, he found what he'd been looking for. Heart pounding, he knelt down, fingered the board. Grabbed the edge and pulled on it slightly. Just to see if there was any give.

There was.

Repositioning his fingers, he grasped the edge again, pulled hard with one forceful yank, and watched the board fall to the ground.

As he leaned down, he told himself a dozen things. Prepared himself to be disappointed. Cautioned himself that Daniel could have very well have lied about everything.

But there, nestled in the cubby, was a small jar with a rusted lid. And inside looked to be a rather large collection of silver coins.

It seemed that for all his bluffing and posturing, Daniel Ropp had not been a rich man after all. The coins were many, and would surely add up to a good amount, but they were in no way the fortune than John had been led to believe was there.

John reached into the cavity, pulled out the jar, and scrambled to his feet. And then did the only thing that was fitting.

He acted far more excited than he was.

Pasting a happy smile on his face, he darted around the corner of the barn and called out her name. "Sarah! Sarah, where are you?"

He found her in the same place he'd left her hours before, standing in the sunlight, carefully pinning articles of clothing on the line.

When she saw what he was holding, the shirt in her hands fluttered down onto the ground. "John, is that what I think it is?"

He nodded. He held up the jar like it was grand prize at a fair. "Can you even believe it?"

She shook her head slowly. "*Nee*, I cannot," she uttered, her voice shaky. "John, I must admit that a part of me thought this was a fool's errand. I didn't think it really existed."

"I promise, there was many a time when I thought the same exact thing. And then, when I got to know you, and learned that Daniel could be so very manipulative, I began to imagine that he'd merely been playing a joke on me." Then he smiled. "But I was wrong."

Slowly, happiness lit her eyes. "This is *wunderbaar*," she whispered as she rushed to his side.

The moment she was in his reach, he tossed the jar on the ground, picked her up by the waist, and twirled her around. And then because it felt so good, he twirled her around a second time.

She rested her hands on his arms and laughed. "I canna believe it!"

With care, he set her back on her feet, then grasped her hand and began to pull her into the house. "I can hardly believe it myself."

"Where was it? I thought you were outside?"

"I was. I was walking around the barn, trying to think of what I had missed—and then it came to me."

"What did?"

"A conversation I'd had with Daniel right before the explosion. He told me that he'd hidden the jar outside near the oak tree."

Her eyes widened as they entered the kitchen. "Is that where it was? Near the bee tree?"

"There was a loose plank near the ground. It didn't look quite right so I gave it a little pull and the thing came right out."

She shook her head in wonder. "I wonder why he would have chosen that spot. He knows how afraid—" She stopped herself just as a look of dismay crossed her features. "That is why he hid it there. Ain't so?"

"Yes." He didn't want to lie to her. But he sure hadn't wanted her to ever know just why Daniel had planted the jar in such a place.

Wearily, she sat down. "I don't know why I'm surprised, but I am. John, he did so many things with the intent to hurt me."

"He was like that with many people, Sarah. He was a selfish man. And, at times, a cruel one."

"I don't know why. That's not our way. It's against everything we are."

He chose his words with care. He didn't want to make her memories of Daniel Ropp any worse than they were and he didn't want to offend her religion in any way, either. "When I was on the battlefield, I saw a great many men from all walks of life, Sarah," he began quietly. "Some were wealthy landowners, some were poor men who came from fishing villages on the New England coast. All of us united for one reason: to fight for a cause we believed in. It was easy to make all Southerners into villains. You're not going to like hearing this, but it made it easier to kill with that mindset."

He paused when she winced, but didn't apologize for his words. War was bloody and painful. It was hard to kill another man, and having to find the wherewithal to do it meant sacrificing a bit of one's humanity.

"Sarah, I'm only telling you this because one day, at the end of a skirmish with a small band of Confederates, I got a pretty good cut on my calf. It had been bleeding something awful, and because of that, I was slow getting up. And that was why I realized that I'd somehow ended up next to an injured Johnny Reb. He was hurt worse than me. He was bleeding from a couple of places. But he was staring at me."

Sarah was staring at him as if mesmerized. "What did you do?"

"I decided to sit with him until he passed." He wouldn't have done that if either had had men from their units there. But in that brief moment of time, they were both alone. "It was an ugly day. Overcast. Chilly. Damp. We were both cold and miserable. I scooted a little closer to him, trying in my own, weak way, I guess, to offer him comfort. He let me because he thought I was dying, too."

Remembering the moment, the way the land had smelled like damp grass and the faint odor of blood and spent ammunition filled the air, he added, "The man had blue eyes."

"Did you say anything?"

"I asked him if he would like me to pray with him."

"Did he let you do that?"

"Uh-huh. He told me about his family. How he was the youngest boy and how his momma was going to be so sad, because she hadn't wanted him to fight in the first place. I told him about growing up without a family. We both agreed it was better to die for something we believed in than for nothing at all. Then we said the Lord's Prayer."

"And then?"

He closed his eyes. "And then he died." Opening his eyes again, he shifted uncomfortably. "After a bit, I tied some of his shirt around my leg, like a tourniquet, and went looking for my camp."

"Did you ever tell anyone about him?"

"No one. Not until you." Realizing he'd gotten off track, he sighed. "Sarah, I don't know if I'm making any sense, but what I'm trying to say is that there's good and bad people in all walks of life. Even Southerners. Even orphans like me. Even a man as fortunate as Daniel, growing up in a caring community like this. There's no telling what makes a man do the things he does. It's a useless exercise to try to figure out why."

At last, Sarah picked up the jar and rolled it in her hands. "I think it's time we saw how much was in here." When she made a move to hand it back to him, he stilled her.

"Nope. This is your moment. You do the honors."

Fifteen

. . . .

The Fulfillment

THE GLASS JAR felt smooth and almost cool in her hands.
The metal top was a bit rusted. As she held it between her
palms, she half expected Daniel to come back from the grave
and chastise her for doing something she shouldn't.

But of course her life had changed.

Glancing at John almost bashfully, she said, "I hardly
know what to do." She paused, instinctively waiting for John
to pull it out of her hands.

But instead, he merely leaned back and smiled. "You can
do it," he murmured. "Just give it a good twist and then we'll
see what's inside."

She didn't bother to let him know that he'd misunderstood her. She wasn't just talking about opening jars; she was
talking about moving forward.

Even the act of holding the jar in her hands felt like she was crossing a bridge. Not just because of the financial change, but because she was finally challenging and overruling her husband's wishes. With one hard pull, she was going to make her own way in the world, doing something for herself instead of abiding by his desires.

The feeling was heady.

In this situation, Daniel hadn't gotten his way. No matter how carefully he'd hidden his money, somehow, someway, the Lord had seen fit to give her a way to be triumphant.

And that felt like a huge accomplishment. And a scary one, too. She knew how to be the downtrodden, almost banished wife of a man many had disagreed with. She'd even gotten used to barely subsisting on her own as a lonely widow.

She wasn't sure how being a triumphant woman was going to fit in her skin—or with the way she thought of herself.

Across from her, John was getting impatient. "Come on, Sarah. Give it a good twist."

She gripped the top and gave it a hard yank, fully expecting it to be sealed tight. But instead it opened with a *pop*. Surprised, she glanced at John. "Could it really have been that easy to open?"

His lips curved up. "You should take a look and see."

She carefully twisted the metal lid and felt a true sense of triumph when she held it in her hands. "I did it!"

John laughed. "Yes, you sure did, Sarah. Now, stop looking at those coins like they're going to reach out and bite you. Take out your money. Let's see what you've got."

She inverted the bottle, gave it a good shake. One silver

dollar after another clattered onto the table with a bright jingle. Then, she had to reach in and pull out the few silver coins that were stuck to the sides. After she gave it another shake, the remaining coins jangled against the sides of the glass jar, before at last settling onto the table with a satisfying *clunk*.

It seemed like a lot of money to her. After all, she'd never had much for most of her life. But John had been led to believe that Daniel had squirreled away a small fortune. This wasn't that. Warily, she lifted her head and gazed at him.

Instead of looking disgruntled, he was staring at the pile of coins with a gleam in his eyes.

"How much do you think all those coins are worth?" she asked.

"We'll have to count them, of course. But I'd have to say it's a fair amount."

"Fair amount" didn't sound all that exciting. "Do you think the amount might be as much as you'd hoped?"

He leaned back. It was obvious that he was attempting to look more relaxed than he truly was. "It doesn't matter how much I thought was going to be hidden. The money is yours anyway. Now, go ahead and count the coins, Sarah."

"We could do it together—"

"We could, but I'd rather watch you do it." Softly, he pushed a couple of the coins closer to her. "Everyone needs a moment like this. Take it."

Understanding what he meant even though she'd never contemplated needing to count a pile of silver in her life, Sarah reached out and made a neat and tidy stack of ten.

"That's ten silver dollars." But as she looked at the seemingly ever-increasing pile of twinkling silver, it didn't look as if she'd made the slightest dent.

"Ten dollars is a real good start." He made a shooing motion with his hands. "But you've a real long way to go. There's a good amount left, don'tcha think?"

"Are you sure you don't you want to help?"

"I'm positive." With a chuckle, he added. "Now come on, or we'll be sitting here all night." And with that, John leaned back and folded his arms over his chest. Both showing and telling her that he didn't intend to take over.

"All right, then." As excitement built inside her, she stacked more coins. Soon, she had three stacks of ten and there was still so much more to go. "This is a grand amount."

He grinned. "Indeed, it is."

"I can't help but wonder how long Daniel was saving it all. To put away this much would take a long time. Ain't so?"

"Years and years. If I had to guess, I'd say at least four or five years." His smile was gone now, and a more serious expression had settled into his features. "It makes me wonder how he accumulated so many coins. I've always been poor, but even I know men don't part with silver easily."

"I couldn't begin to imagine." With a sigh, she formed another stack, making forty dollars counted. "Almost done now."

"You are the only person who would sound relieved about this."

"I'm not relieved. I simply feel a little awkward. John, I had no idea this much was hiding in the barn." Privately, she also couldn't help but remember all the times she'd gone without things, believing Daniel when he'd told her that they hadn't gotten as much money for their wheat or grain or corn as she'd thought.

Or when he'd come home from visiting the Englischer's store without the fabric she'd asked for. The fabric he'd offered to buy for her . . . but then had acted like she'd been terrible to accept.

When she set the very last coin in order, she gazed at the shiny silver stacks in awe. "That is sixty dollars."

Picking up two lone coins, he said, "Sixty-two, to be exact."

"That's a great deal of money."

"Yes it is. Is there something you've been wanting to buy?"

There was so much. She'd always longed to have a wagon to carry supplies. Or . . . maybe a pig or a goat. Or both! And then there was the opportunity to buy grain and seeds for a real garden. Better farm implements. So many things!

But now, as she stared at the coins, it occurred to her that John's only reason for remaining with her was gone. One day soon she would wake up alone. Make breakfast for one and tend to her animals and the farm all by herself.

Soon, she wouldn't have anyone to talk to, anyone to laugh with. She would simply be an Amish widow with a mystery about her, getting older year after year.

Suddenly, the stacks of coins no longer felt very special.

In fact, nothing felt all that special. "I think I'd best do some thinking about how to spend all this money," she said at last, knowing as she did that her statement didn't ring true.

After gazing at her for a long moment, John stood up. "You know what? I think that's a real fine idea. No hurry, is there?" Giving the coins another look of concern, he added, "You might want to not spend them all at one time. Folks might get to wondering why you are suddenly spending those silver coins if you haven't before."

"*Danke*," with false brightness. "That . . . that is good advice."

The muscles in his neck tightened as silence enveloped the room. Abruptly, he clapped his hands together. "I think it's time I washed up and got my things together."

"So soon?" A cold knot formed in her stomach as she sprang to her feet. "You're not planning to leave this evening, are you?"

"I think it would be for the best."

He was right, she supposed. No good could ever come from them pretending to be something they weren't. No good could ever come from him taking Daniel's identity. To do so would surely shame them both.

It would be a sin. A terrible sin.

And it would besmirch Daniel's memory. He might have had his faults, but the Lord knew they all did. And she was certainly filled with her fair share of flaws.

But, as John turned, she thought about being alone again. Thought about hearing leaves rustle outside her window in the middle of the night and sitting up in fright. Waiting to be attacked.

Thought about being a near castoff in her community. About how she'd carried the burden of her husband's decision while no one had really taken the time to think about her. Or to ask her how they could help her. Instead, she'd felt more alone than ever before. And worse, she'd felt as if she'd had no way out.

Then she realized her shame would be complete if everyone thought that her husband had found her to be so unworthy that he'd chosen to leave her. Why, she would likely never recover from that embarrassment.

But more than any of that, she thought about her growing fondness for John. How she was beginning to trust him, when she hadn't trusted any man for most of her life. She thought about how one smile from him could light up her day. And how one gentle compliment carried so much weight that she gripped it tightly to her chest like it was worth a fortune.

The truth was that she cared for him. She cared for him like a woman cared for a man. A sweetheart cared for her beau. A wife cared for her husband.

And that was when the muscles tightened inside her, and she realized that she truly could never let him go.

She rushed forward. "John, wait." When he didn't seem to hear her, she raised her voice, not even caring that panic laced her tone now. "Wait!"

He turned, confusion marking his brow. "What do you need?"

That was always what he did, she realized. He put her needs before his.

Now that he was staring at her, his gaze searching, she felt herself color. What she was about to suggest was inappropriate and bordering on being a Jezebel.

But she couldn't help herself. The alternative was too dear. Of that, she was certain. "John, what if you stayed here longer?"

"What are you saying?"

"What if . . . what if you don't leave soon? What if you stayed awhile?" What she ached to add but didn't were the rest of her thoughts. What if he didn't leave, ever? What if he stayed by her forever?

Even thinking such things should make her feel ashamed. But instead, all she felt was hope.

A muscle in his cheek jumped, as if he was doing everything he possibly could to stay in control. "If I stay, there would always be the worry in the back of our minds that someone might find out about us."

"I don't see how anyone would ever know. No one would doubt my word."

"But some already suspect. If those suspicions continue, it will cause talk."

"I've survived gossip, John. And I daresay you've survived worse."

"That I have," he murmured. For the briefest of seconds, his gaze settled on her. Just before a line of red traipsed up his neck. "I must admit as well, that there's something else to consider. See, if I stay here with you, other problems might arise."

"I don't follow."

He kept his gaze averted. "I mean between you and me, Sarah. You are a lovely woman. A virtuous woman. I am very far from a saint. Eventually I'm afraid I would ask you for more than you might want to give." He cleared his throat. "I would never hurt you, of course. I would never force myself on you. But if something happened? Well, we wouldn't truly be married."

She stepped backward. She hadn't thought about anything like that. However, she wasn't sure if it was the idea of him one day coming into her bedroom that made her uneasy, or if it was the idea that he never would.

"I'm sure we could discuss that in the future." She couldn't even believe she was talking like this. Thinking like this! She wasn't a loose woman. She wasn't without morals. But she'd also known what it was like to be with a man who had broken his vows.

And she knew what it was like to feel as if she would always be alone.

John looked overcome. "Sarah, I'm afraid to guess at what you are thinking. You're going to have to be a little more clear."

Now she was embarrassed. "I guess I'm asking if you would consider staying here. With everyone thinking you were Daniel."

"For how long?" His voice was harsh with tension.

The idea of him leaving was painful. And the change in her feelings was something she was going to need to examine. "I guess I am suggesting you would stay as long as you wanted."

"And what would we become? Sarah, you heard everything I just said. What would we be?"

Stunned, she stared at him. And what she saw almost

made her heart stop beating. "This time you are going to have to be the one who speaks clearly, John."

"I'm saying that if I stay, what would I be to you? Your husband? Your boarder?"

It wasn't her place to say, was it? To make such assumptions would be wrong. But he was asking for her opinion . . . and it was time to stand up for herself. Past time. "Perhaps you could simply be my partner?"

The tightening muscle in his jaw told her what he thought of her vague reply. "I could be that, Sarah. I could be your secret partner. For a while. But not forever. Not for years."

His answer puzzled her. "But we would still be working together," she murmured.

"That is true." He inhaled, seeming to come to a decision. "You see, I'm only a man. One day I know being just your partner and workmate won't be enough. I will want more than that."

"More?" She honestly wasn't sure what he was referring to. He would have the land, the property. Even the silver. What more could he want?

A flush stained his cheeks as he lowered his voice, finally replying. "Sarah, one day, us being partners is not going to be enough for me. I . . . I would want to be your husband in truth, not just in name only." He paused, obviously wanting his meaning to sink in. "I think you are lovely, Sarah. I desire you. One day, I'm going to want children. A family. But I'm not sure if that is what you are ever going to want. If you don't think you're ever going to want me in that way, you're going to need to let me know."

"John—" She didn't know what to say, but surely she had to say something!

He held up a hand. "I don't need an answer this second. But I needed to put it out there. It needed to be said. So, do some thinking about all that before you ask me to stay. Think about it long and hard. Because once we make this decision there will be no going back."

She watched him turn and walk out the door, feeling like she was out of breath again. When the door slammed shut, she reached out and grasped the edge of the table and used it to support herself as she sat back down again.

Memories of Daniel coming to her bed clashed with the feelings of longing she'd entertained when John had held her hand. When he'd looked at her a certain way.

When he'd wrapped his arms around her, offering his support.

Instinctively, she knew that an intimate relationship with John would be different from the only one she'd known. Everything about him was kinder, gentler. More patient.

How could she knowingly invite him to enter such a relationship?

But if she didn't, how could she send him away?

And only when she caught her breath did she dare ask herself why she was so stunned and scared. Was it because everything she had been afraid of was finally going to happen?

Or was it that everything she'd wished for might actually come true?

Was it his question that had discomfited her? Or, rather, her answer to it?

Sixteen

· · · · · · · · ·

The New Plan

BEFORE THE SUN had done much more than peek out over the horizon, Sarah was up and dressed and opening her bedroom door. It was time to face her fears and discuss everything with John. And the best time to do that, she knew, was in the early morning hours.

Walking past the sofa, she peeked over, intending to gauge how sound asleep he was so she would know how much time she had to prepare her speech.

And then she realized the sofa was empty again.

For the first time since he'd arrived, he'd left a mess. His pillow lay on the floor, his pair of quilts were rumpled and pulled back in a jumbled heap on the edge of the cushion.

It was obvious that he'd left in a hurry.

Panic filled her. Had she scared him with her proposal?

Had he waited until she'd gone to sleep in a mess of tears and worries? If so, she knew he was gone forever from her life. There was no way she could search for him, especially since she was afraid to tell anyone his real name.

"John?" she called out, though she knew that was a foolish idea. It was obvious he wasn't in the small room.

She breathed a sigh of relief when she spied his saddlebag resting against the wall. She knew now, at the very least, that he hadn't gone far.

Carelessly throwing a knitted shawl over her shoulders, she rushed outside to the barn. Breathing carefully only when she saw that the barn door was opened slightly.

Surely that meant he was inside. Maybe he was doing chores? Maybe he simply needed some time and space to consider things?

If she went inside, what would she say? Was she willing to give her speech now?

"What are you doing out here dressed like that?" a rough voice suddenly said, as an arm snaked out and pulled her into the dark confines of the barn.

"John!" she cried out as she stumbled.

"You're going to catch your death, running outside in your bare feet."

"I only came out to look for you. I was afraid you'd left." Realizing that his hoarse tone sprang from worry and not anger, she gently released her arm from his grip. "Why are you out here?"

His gaze searched hers. "Last night was a pretty big day. I couldn't sleep."

"Were you thinking about the coins?"

"Actually, it was last night's conversation that had me tossing and turning."

"I came out here to talk to you about that."

He paused, then looked at her again and frowned. And then, before she even knew what he was about, he picked her up.

One of his hands was under her knees, the other firmly around her shoulder blades. Every inch of her left side pressed against his body as he carried her back to the house. She couldn't remember ever being carried before. She batted his shoulder with a hand. "John, what in the world?"

"We are not going to have a conversation with you freezing. And I'm not going to let you walk back alone."

"But, John—"

"And Sarah, that's another thing," he said as he pushed open the door with the brunt of his shoulder then carried her across the threshold. "You're going to have to stop calling me John all the time."

As her feet touched the floor, she felt her knees threaten to give way. She was that confounded by what she was hearing. "Why would I need to stop calling you by your Christian name?" she whispered.

"I think you know."

"I think you'd better tell me."

He tilted his head so their eyes met. "Well, it's like this. I can think of a dozen reasons why leaving you is the right thing to do." A flash of pain entered his eyes before his expression cleared. "But the fact of the matter is this: I simply don't think I can."

While she tried to understand what he was saying, he continued. "Sarah, the only honorable thing Jonathan Scott did in his life was become an officer in the Union army by the skin of his teeth. I figure maybe it's time I gave that name a break and slipped another identity on for size."

"You're willing to stay here as my husband? As Daniel?"

"I've already started this sham. I can't bear to have everyone think I up and left you." As his words hung in the air, he shook his head. "No, I'm going to stop doing that. I'm going to stop pretending I'm only thinking of you here. The truth of the matter is that I don't want to leave you. I'd like have a home and a wife and a life." He paused, blinked, then added, "And I also like the way you look at me."

"How do I do that?"

"You look at me as if I matter, Sarah. I can't get enough of that. So, if you still want me, I want to stay."

She'd wondered until this very second if she'd actually be able to go through with the plan. She had wondered if she'd be willing to put everything she was to one side in order to live for everything she thought she wanted.

But the other options seemed so insurmountable. If he admitted to everyone that he'd pretended to be Daniel, he would not only be hated but everyone would suppose that they'd been living in sin.

If they left, she would lose her home, and even a money jar full of coins couldn't pay for the beginnings of a new life.

Indeed, every other option seemed like they'd be going down a road full of hardship and pain.

Or they could simply continue a lie. At least for a little while. Until they discovered another option. "Stay, Daniel."

He looked shaken. Almost stunned. And then, wonder of wonders, he smiled. "You feel like making breakfast this morning, Sarah? Because suddenly, I feel like I could eat a horse."

"I'll start making the coffee right now."

"I'll go outside then and wash up." Before she could say another word, he walked out the door and closed it behind him.

Leaving her almost breathless as she realized what they'd just decided.

AS SOON AS he knew for sure that he was out of Sarah's eyesight, John leaned his head against the house and closed his eyes.

It was over.

He'd gotten everything he wanted. So why did it feel like he'd come up on the losing side of a bloody battle? His insides felt weak and sore. Empty.

It was because he wanted to be worthy of her. Pretending to be her abusive husband wasn't something that set well with him. And though he already knew he would cherish her for the rest of his days, he hated the thought of pretending to be a man who had hurt her in so many ways.

There was also one small point that he was reluctant to admit to himself—now that he was giving up his name for all intents and purposes, he felt a true sense of loss. While it was true that Jonathan Scott hadn't been all that much, it had been who he was. Now it felt as if he had finally taken the side of all the people who'd made him feel less than human. As if he'd finally given up on John Scott, too.

It was a funny thing, survival. He'd learn at a young age that it made a man do things he never thought he would. When he was younger, living at the orphanage, and then later with different families working for room and board but without love or affection, he realized he could subsist on very little. It was all a matter of either living or dying.

And dying had always seemed like such a permanent thing.

Later, in the war, he'd gotten a taste of what it was to be just like everyone else. When he'd first donned that Union uniform and had looked around at the other men, he'd felt included for the first time in his life. He'd enjoyed the feeling of having clothes that weren't another person's hand-me-downs. He'd liked fitting in.

Those first weeks in the training camp had been a world of wonder, too. He'd discovered that a lifetime of being quicker, tougher, and meaner had served him well. He'd followed orders with ease and had distinguished himself in front of the officers. So much so that a major had claimed him and taken him under his wing.

And then the other men began to look to him for direction. That measure of respect had been a revelation. After a lifetime of feeling unwanted, he'd become worthy. When he'd gotten burned in the fire, he'd been discharged. And with that, everything he'd gained in self-esteem vanished. Once again, he'd been alone in the world. Though the major had kindly reminded him he deserved to go home and rest, John had known he had no home to return to and no family to see.

He'd imagined he would spend the rest of his life alone and unneeded. But to his amazement, it looked as if the Lord was going to give him another opportunity to shine. And because of that, he was willing to work harder, to try harder to become the man Sarah Ropp needed him to be.

Her needs and wants were important to him. The longer he got to know her, the more he was aware of how poorly she'd been treated by Daniel. She needed to have someone to lean on.

She needed to feel valued and special.

With that in mind, John washed his face in a rush then walked back inside just as she was putting their eggs on the table with thick slices of bread she'd toasted in the oven.

"We're celebrating today with three eggs?"

"I figure it's a pretty grand occasion. And now that we have some coins, I'm hoping we can get another couple of hens."

Her small request humbled him. "We should go into town today. Or I will, if you'd rather. We'll get some things at the general store that you've been missing, like flour and grain for the animals."

"And can we stop at the Yosts' farm on the way home to see about the hens?"

"Of course we can." He smiled at her gently. "Is there anything else you'd like to buy right now?"

"Not yet. What about you?"

He wanted a horse, but that would take most of the funds. "Nothing yet." Fingering his clothes, he said, "Well, maybe some cloth? I'd like some clothes that fit."

Her expression softened. "I would be happy to make you some."

He smiled at her, remembering how skittish he'd been when she'd been attempting to make him his shirt. They'd circled each other like a pair of nervous nellies, each afraid of saying what was really on their minds.

He could hardly believe they'd come so far.

At last, he made his last, most important request. "Sarah, about the two of us . . ."

She stilled. "Yes?"

He wiped his hands on his trousers, realizing his palms had suddenly gone damp. "Well, I hope that we could also get a license."

"For what?"

"I'm speaking of a marriage license." When her blue eyes widened, he rushed to explain, hating that his voice was betraying his nervousness, allowing her to realize just how much he wanted to be legally married. Forever. "Ah, it doesn't have to be right now. But perhaps, we could marry one day. When you are ready."

"I've never imagined a wedding among the English."

She sounded shocked, and he didn't blame her. But he also knew that she was going to have to be willing to put some of her fears to the side if their new partnership was ever going to work. "I know it's not the best situation, but I think there are some benefits to that idea."

"But I wouldn't know what to do. How to act?"

"All you'd have to do is be yourself. I'd take care of the rest," he promised. Though he knew his words were going to make her uncomfortable, he plowed ahead. "We can't marry here, can we? But I think it would be best for us both to be legally wed."

"All right, John," she murmured.

Her voice was restrained. Afraid she was feeling bullied, he wondered how he was ever going to make things better. Wondered what he could ever say to convey the wealth of his emotions.

Then he noticed the light shining in her eyes.

And realized that she, too, was just as excited as he was.

Seventeen

A Hero's Welcome

ANOTHER SUNDAY WAS upon them.

As Sarah carefully checked her stockings for runs and pinned on her apron, she found it hard to believe that a whole month had already passed.

Every time Sarah reflected on the last thirty days, she couldn't help but shake her head in wonder. For the last three years, time had seemed to be at a standstill. Morning would fade into night, then shift from restless sleep to a new dawn that would sluggishly arise. Some days had felt like whole weeks, some hours like an eternity.

Now, she greeted each day with a hope-filled smile and end each night with a prayer of gratitude. John's appearance in her life had changed her life completely. He was a true helpmate, a man who brought her smiles. He'd even taught her to find joy and humor in most any situation. He'd taught her how to laugh at herself—and at him. What they had made her days suddenly feel worthwhile again. She was so grateful for his friendship and his trust.

All that was why she'd at last agreed to be his wife.

Though they still hadn't talked of love, she'd lived long enough to know that some things were more important than flowery words. These were the things that John had given her: trust, friendship, laughter, and the knowledge that she was no longer going to have to wake up each morning with the uneasy feeling that she was completely alone.

Two weeks ago, she'd nervously accompanied him on the long journey to Mansfield. They'd borrowed a neighbor's horse, choosing to purchase a small wagon along the way. Once they were in the outskirts of the town, she'd carefully removed her *kapp* and put on the new calico he'd bought her. Though wearing clothes out of her faith felt wrong, she agreed with John that it would be best to not draw attention to themselves. The last thing they needed was for word to get back to her church community that she had married "Daniel" in a county courthouse.

As they stood outside the front door of the imposing government building, John had turned to her and taken her hand. "Are you sure about this? I don't want you to have any regrets."

"I'm sure. I want to be your wife, John. Your wife in truth."

After gazing at her a moment longer, he'd nodded and held out his arm for her to take. Curving her hand around his arm, they'd entered as Sarah Ropp, widow of fallen soldier Daniel Ropp, and Lieutenant Jonathan Scott.

It had taken practically no time for John to complete the paperwork and pay the fee. Then, in front of a weary judge and two disinterested clerks, they'd exchanged solemn vows.

Suddenly, it hadn't mattered that they were dressed in English clothes and standing in the midst of strangers. All that really mattered to Sarah was the look of happiness she spied when she gazed into John's eyes.

Instinctively, she knew he meant every word when he'd promised to love and cherish her. And when she said those words, she'd felt as if all the years of hardship before him had suddenly melted away.

Which was why their brief ceremony had felt both exactly right and terribly wrong. She understood the need for them to be legally bound, and had understood the reasons for her to legally be Mrs. Jonathan Scott.

But becoming his wife in such a secular, foreign building, without the support and love of friends and relatives, had felt strange.

And because there was no mention of the Lord in the secular ceremony, because she wasn't even sure if she could one day fall in love, the event had felt a bit hollow.

She had sorely needed the Lord to be with her on such an important day, for she surely felt He had been behind the miraculous changes that had taken place in her life.

When she'd mentioned such a thing to John, he'd wrapped one strong arm around her shoulders . . . and then had told her she was being foolish.

"Of course the Lord is with us, Sarah. He brought us together, didn't He?"

"Well, *jah*. But—"

"All we need to remember is that He is with us in our hearts. God didn't need to be mentioned in the ceremony by that judge, Sarah. He knows of our faith."

That had been all she'd needed to hear to remember that marrying John had been the exactly right thing to do.

Now, a full two weeks after their ceremony, not much had changed between them. John remained carefully respectful and always kind and patient. She was learning to be more comfortable around him, but she didn't feel as if she could completely let down her guard yet.

John still slept on the sofa while she continued to close the bedroom door firmly each night.

But as the days passed, they lingered over their partings. Sometimes John even reached out and pressed his palm against hers. Once he'd glided two fingers along the curve of her cheek.

Most recently she'd taken to standing against her door after they parted, feeling strangely bereft. Once, she'd even fantasized about the day when their separate sleeping arrangements were a thing of the past.

For his part, John seemed to take her reticence in stride, often reminding her that he was willing to wait weeks and months if that was what she needed. It seemed he was worried about causing her further pain.

However, it didn't look as if the waiting was all that easy for him, either. Sometimes she caught him staring at her face a moment longer than he had before. Now and then he'd taken to resting his hand on the small of her back when they were walking from the barn to the house. When she'd asked him why he'd done such a thing, he'd chuckled.

"It's one of the few manners I learned, I suppose," he said somewhat sheepishly. "A gentleman is supposed to guide his lady."

"Why?"

"I guess so she feels like someone is looking after her." He'd shrugged. "Do you mind my touch, Sarah?"

She'd felt her cheeks heat as she shook her head. No, she didn't mind his touch at all. She'd even begun to look forward to it—not that she would ever admit that to him.

But it seemed as if that small exchange had emboldened him.

Just that evening his fingers had brushed hers when she'd handed him a dish of cornbread. And his gaze had seemed a little more thoughtful, a little bit warmer when he relaxed next to her on the sofa. For a moment she'd considered asking him what he was about. But simply sitting next to him had felt too nice and comfortable to question things further. They'd spent at least an hour simply sitting together, not talking all that much.

Mainly they just spent time basking in the peace that had come from the knowledge that all the secrets and doubts between them had been laid to rest.

They'd even begun to mix with the other Amish in her church community. Little by little, other men began to joke with him and other women stopped giving him such a wide berth. At first everyone was wary because he was so different. And the scars put people off, too. But soon John's kind nature began to shine through their reticence.

John enjoyed being around people and therefore Sarah knew he was glad that everyone was willing to give "Daniel" a second chance. But Sarah also realized that the ruse sometimes left him exhausted. Hearing some of the stories about Daniel's past—about the man everyone assumed he still was—was also difficult for him. She was discovering that if there was anything that was guaranteed to put her husband in a foul mood, it was hearing a story about Daniel's mistreatment of her.

It was that thought that spurred her to double-check with John about their plans to attend church that morning. The air was cold and drizzling. Both were things that made his injuries ache.

"Are you sure you don't mind attending church?" she asked as he helped her wrap her black shawl around her head and dress. "I know your arm is paining you something awful."

He bent his right arm experimentally. "It does pain me on days like today, when the weather is damp and cold, but the doctor promised that it would, likely for quite some time. The nerves were damaged and some are trying to repair themselves, whatever that means."

He frowned as he ran one smooth finger down the discolored and uneven skin that covered the knuckles of his right hand. "The new skin is soft while the old, damaged skin is tight and calloused, I fear. Perhaps the two are trying to get used to each other, just as we have been. I'm just sorry you have to look at it."

"I like how you look."

His chuckle was low and strained. "I'd call you a liar if I didn't already know you were anything but that."

"It's true, John. When I see your scars, it reminds me of how brave you were. And it reminds me how you are most definitely not Daniel."

"I'd like to think I was as brave as any other man on the battlefield, but we both know my scars came from a simple explosion in our compound, not from a feat of bravery."

When he spoke like that, she became even more fond of him. Daniel would have spun a story to explain his wounds. He would have been unable to resist such a thing.

But John never glorified himself or his battles. Not beyond a steady pride that he had served with honor.

She ached to ease his hurt. Impulsively, she reached for his hand and clasped it in between hers. With smooth strokes, she rubbed the skin along his knuckles, caressing the damaged skin along his wrist and forearm.

His eyes closed for a brief moment, his expression full of bliss. "Your touch feels so good. Thank you."

"No thanks are needed, John. I want to help you. You know what? We have some liniment in the barn. I used it for the horse when she hurt her leg. Perhaps we could try rubbing a bit of that on your arm and hand? I think maybe the oils might help your skin become more pliable."

"I'm willing to try anything." Carefully he stretched his fingers a bit. "I don't know that I'll ever be able to use my hand all that well, but any improvement would be a welcome change."

She felt terrible. She'd been so focused on his return and all their emotional hurdles, she'd scarcely taken time to remember that he was an injured man who had barely survived a terrible explosion and fire. "I'll rub some of the salve on you this evening then."

"*Danke*, Sarah," he said after slipping on his own coat, the one that now fit him well, thanks to the bolts of material they'd bought in Mansfield and her time with a needle and thread. "And thank you for the coat, too. It is very fine."

"I will make another pair of pants for you soon."

"I'd rather you make something for yourself." Reaching out, he brushed a finger against her cheek. "There's a reason we bought that bolt of blue wool, remember."

His words sounded so loving, his gaze was so kind, she felt her cheeks heat. Unsure of how to respond to such things, she tucked her chin.

He chuckled. "Well, we should probably go now. We don't want to be late."

"I hope you will fare all right."

"I survived last time. I will survive again."

"I know it is difficult for you, not knowing the language well."

"I need to learn my Pennsylvania Dutch better. Besides, worshipping with your friends and neighbors makes you happy, Sarah. And if you're happy, then I am, too."

"I do love worshipping, but I don't want you to be uncomfortable."

"I won't be. Besides, I enjoy spending time with the Lord. Heaven knows I've called on Him a whole lot over the last couple of years." With a teasing grin, he ran one hand down the front of his coat. "Besides, I'll get to show off my new coat today."

She couldn't help but smile back at him. "You will look mighty handsome, for sure and for certain."

He looked away, obviously embarrassed. "We both know I'll never be that. But thank you."

Then, to her surprise, he leaned close and carefully pressed his lips to her cheek before quickly turning away. It was all she could do to not cradle her cheek in the palm of her hand the whole way to the Millers' farm.

They arrived right on time.

To her disconcertion, Zeke was the first person they came into contact with. Feeling awkward, she'd been tempted to simply tuck her chin and keep walking. But John was made of sterner stuff.

"Zeke, it's *gut* to see you," he said, just as if things hadn't been left so badly between them.

After looking in her direction for a moment, Zeke straightened his shoulders. "It's *gut* to see you both as well."

"Could you give me some advice? I intend to go to horse auction soon but I've got a couple of concerns."

"Of course, Daniel. What are you worried about?"

Sarah smiled softly as John began doing what he did best, quietly breaking down barriers. By the time they reached the rest of the congregation, John and Zeke were talking about horses and auctions like two long-lost friends.

Satisfied that her husband was going to be just fine, Sarah left John's side and joined the other women, who were gathered around a new baby.

As she walked toward them, several of the women called out to her and smiled cheerfully. Sarah returned the greetings with pleasure, her heart practically singing.

Finally, she was a happily married wife. At long last, she fit in with the others. It was as if everyone in the community found her more approachable now. Perhaps it was because she felt more eager to be around others. When she was married to Daniel she'd been too beaten down to do much more than get through each day as best she could. Later, when she was widowed, her circumstances had distanced her even further from the others.

Now, as she entered the Millers' barn with two of the women, she was pleased to see many others motioning for her to sit by their sides.

It was surely amazing that it took an Englischer to help her become a true part of her Amish community.

Of course she knew that if anyone discovered her secrets and lies she would most likely be shunned. She would deserve everyone's disdain, too. But until that happened, she kept telling herself that the only person she and John owed an explanation to was the Lord.

She knew He wasn't one to appreciate lying, but she also had to imagine that the Lord likely wasn't all that happy with men who abused their wives, either. Sarah hoped that He wouldn't mind her finding happiness after being through so much.

After the men and the few last scalawags traipsed in and seated themselves on the benches, the preacher began his sermon.

Jeremiah was preaching today, and a more respected man in their midst she couldn't name. He was in his sixties and could claim a dozen children and three times that many grandchildren. He was known to be a thoughtful and serious man. A mighty wise one, too.

As he spoke about Moses and his many trials, Sarah tried her best to concentrate on his words. But more often than not, her gaze slowly drifted across the aisle and settled on John. She'd notice the way his chin was tilted or the way he was holding himself, wondering if the skin along his torso bothered him as much as his hands. Each time, his eyes would meet hers, almost as if he could sense her attention.

Then, to her happiness, his gaze would settle on hers for a long moment, and it would feel as if they were the only two people in the room.

"I can't help but notice your Daniel is actin' like a new-lywed," Esther whispered into Sarah's ear about halfway through the service. "You are, too, if I'm not mistaken." When Sarah's cheeks heated, the other woman laughed softly. "I wouldn't mind receiving a few of those heated looks a time or two. Maybe I should send my man off for three years."

"I wouldn't recommend it," Sarah said lightly, then, after once again sharing a small smile with John, she turned her attention to Jeremiah's sermon.

As another hour passed, and their younger preacher, Abraham, began to speak, she found herself already anticipating riding by John's side on their trip home. Perhaps this time he would reach for her hand. And perhaps this time she would let him hold it.

Imagining such a thing made her pulse race. If she held his hand in between her own, she could pretend that she only wanted to ease his sore skin. When, really, she just wanted to feel his fingers linked with hers.

At last the service was over. After giving thanks in a private prayer, Sarah stood up and stretched. Just as they all began to file out of the warm barn, a commotion arose among the folks standing near the barn's entrance. Gasps were followed by cries of joy as everyone appeared to gather around a newcomer. Immediately, the people closest to the open door crowded closer, blocking everyone else's view of whatever was happening.

Sarah and the women hurried into the aisle, hoping to catch a glimpse of what had so many people so excited. Unfortunately, she was more petite than the other women around her. No matter how hard she craned her neck, she couldn't see a thing.

Unable to hold her tongue, she asked excitedly. "What has made everyone so glad of heart? Who is here?"

Esther was a few inches taller and used her height to peek around the assemblage. Then she gasped. "Praise the Lord! Oh, Sarah. It's a wonder, is what it is."

"What, exactly, is a wonder?"

"Lloyd Mast is standing in the doorway! He's returned from the war!"

"Lloyd is back?" Surely she hadn't heard correctly!

"*Jah!* Lloyd Mast! We all thought he had died, but it seems the stories we heard about his death were wrong. Oh, Sarah, it is surely a miracle and a wonder, too. Lloyd, like your Daniel, has returned to us all!"

Shock reverberated through her as the implications settled in. Never had she imagined that any of the other six men had also survived. John had certainly made it seem as if no one else had.

While others rushed forward, she darted to the side, searching the throng of men, looking for John. At last she spied him at the back of the crowd. His mouth was set in a thin line. She practically ran to his side. "What are we going to do?" she asked as soon as they were standing alone.

"I'm not sure. I'm worried I've misunderstood what they are saying. Are they speaking of Lloyd Mast?"

After darting a glance around them to make sure they weren't being overheard, she nodded. "Lloyd is another Amish man who became a soldier," she whispered. "He left with Daniel."

His expression turned bleak. "That's what I feared I had heard."

"Feared? Do you recognize his name? Have you met him?" Her stomach dropped.

"Yes." Looking regretful, he looked her in the eyes. "Sarah, I'm afraid I do know Lloyd."

Little by little, she felt her world crumble. Through a gap in the crowd, she saw several men gesture toward her husband. It was obvious now that they were telling Lloyd about Daniel's return. "Do . . . do you think he remembers you?"

"I would be surprised if he did not. For three months, several companies were all gathered together for training. I recognize Lloyd because we all knew who were the Amish men in our midst. I'm afraid he might recognize me, on account of my rank. I was one of the company's lieutenants. Most of the men reported to me."

Scrambling for salvation, she blurted, "Maybe you knew a different Lloyd. It's a common enough name . . ."

"I doubt there were two Amish men with the same name, Sarah."

"What do you think he's going to say? Do you think he'll believe you are Daniel?" Her words spun together, she was so anxious to keep things the way they were. To keep things perfect.

"Maybe he will, maybe he won't." With a grim expression, he gestured to the almost empty aisle. "We won't know until we go forward. And it is time to do that."

But still, she hung back. Anxious to delay the inevitable. "But I thought everyone who was in the tent with you perished."

His expression turned gentle. "He wasn't in my tent, Sarah. I had thought Lloyd died weeks before on the battlefield."

"I think everyone is telling him about your return. If he does recognize you, what do you think he will do?" she whispered, hating that she was hoping to further the lies. Hating that she was not sparing a thought of praise for Lloyd's miraculous appearance and was only thinking of her selfish wants and fears.

"I don't know, Sarah." He smiled slightly, though it was strained, showing her that he was just as affected by the sudden change in their life as she was. "We'll get through it, though. With the Lord's help, we will."

She knew the Lord would help her, but she also felt that maybe God needed a nudge. They needed to figure something out! "But, John, what if—"

"Sarah, we won't know anything until we greet him. And we need to greet him," he interrupted. "Already people are looking back at us with concern."

Tears formed in her eyes. "I don't care. I don't want to move." But that wasn't quite right, either. The truth was that she was afraid to move. Afraid to step out of the dim barn and into the bright light of the day—and the future.

"I know you're worried, but it will be okay." Reaching out, he swiped one of her tears with the pad of his thumb. And gentled his voice. "Don't forget, at the end of the day, nothing has changed, Sarah. We are still married."

"I know." But she didn't feel as positive about that as he did. After all, something had changed in his expression. It was wary now. Shuttered.

And it matched the way she was feeling inside. She was afraid of so much. Afraid for John to be recognized, afraid that their sham would be revealed to the whole church community.

Afraid that everything that had begun to form between herself and Jonathan would dissolve in an instant.

"Come now," he muttered. "We can't tarry any longer."

Slowly, they walked down the aisle toward the crowd that

was gathered just outside the doorway. The earlier jubilation she'd heard had passed, and awaiting them now was an expectant silence. Curious, she looked around.

And was stunned to see more than one person looking at her husband with an odd mixture of wariness and distrust.

Sarah felt her body began to tremble. She longed to run away but she had no choice but to continue forward by John's side. If she'd felt she could have, she would have reached for John's hand and grasped it. Anything to give herself support. Her mind spun, frantically rolling around words to spout. But for some reason, nothing came to mind.

Then John stepped forward with a grin and a burst of confidence that was so like Daniel she wondered why she had ever thought his duplicity would be discovered.

"Lloyd," he said, "praise the Lord. You've returned."

Collectively, the crowd inhaled.

Then time seemed to slow as Lloyd gaped at John. First his expression was one of shock, then slowly his eyes narrowed. He turned his head slightly to look at Sarah, then focused on John again. His frown deepened, as did the lines around his eyes. "It's you," he said.

Which told Sarah everything she needed to know. Lloyd knew the man by her side wasn't Daniel. And furthermore, he knew John's true identity.

The air thickened as the tension increased. Sarah's heart was pounding so loudly, she feared everyone could hear it.

Still betraying nothing, John spoke again. "I had heard you'd died during our last skirmish. I am glad that news was in error."

At last, Lloyd spoke. "I was shot, but by the grace of God, I survived. *Jah*, I am grateful to the Lord for seeing me through. The Lord God is good."

John nodded. "Indeed, the Lord is wondrous. Almighty."

"Indeed he is," Lloyd replied. "He watched over me during my years among the English. He kept me safe when I was in battles. He was my guiding light and my rock in times of trouble."

John nodded. "He spared my life as well, and for that, I am grateful."

Lloyd narrowed his eyes, seemed to come to a decision, then raised his voice. "He is many things, and He is all-knowing. He knows—as do I—that you are most definitely not Sarah's husband, Daniel."

Several women gasped.

A cry fell from Sarah's lips before she could stifle it. Dread filled her every pore as she ached to pull John to her side and simply run away.

But next to her, John stood straight and tall. Seeming to ignore her panic. Then, miraculously, with more than a bit of disdain, he said, "Lloyd, I fear you are letting my burns and scars get the best of you. I know I am an ugly man now, and that they are difficult to overlook. But I promise you this: Underneath the scars, I am still the same man."

The tension in the assemblage increased. Sarah's palms began to sweat.

"I believe that to be true, Lieutenant Scott."

While John faced Lloyd stoically, Jeremiah folded his arms across his chest. "Explain yourself, Lloyd," he said.

As the crowd edged closer and several men sought to defend John, Lloyd raised his voice. "I was injured on the battlefield. After mostly recovering from my wounds, I had just returned to our unit when the explosion erupted in your tent. I was close enough to see Daniel's body among the dead. And observant enough to hear that our fierce Lieutenant Scott had sustained terrible burns but was still alive."

Several now looked harder at her husband, their expressions twisting between shock and dismay.

But still John held his ground. Placing his hands on his hips, he said, "There were many of us in that tent. I find it difficult to believe that you know so much about what happened."

"After the explosion, everything was in disarray. After burying the dead, the men that were left were ordered to march south." Lloyd grimaced. "It was a difficult journey. Disease spread through the ranks and I ended up in another hospital, half delirious with fever. Only three weeks ago was I able to head home."

Jeremiah stepped forward, raised his hands, and gently waved them in the air, both claiming the crowd's attention and calming the brewing apprehension. "Tossing accusations about is not our way."

"Neither is assuming other people's identities," Lloyd countered.

Jeremiah looked pained. He breathed in deeply before replying. "Lloyd, we are grateful to the Lord that you have survived. It is an answer to many prayers. Let us move away from the doorway now and enjoy the bountiful feast Martha Miller has provided for us."

Several people in the back nodded and started to turn away.

But to everyone's surprise, Lloyd shook his head. "*Nee*. I aim to put things to rights. Now. We have an imposter in our midst. It needs to be corrected."

Sarah was shaking like a leaf but she knew what had to be done. "Lloyd, you are forgetting that this is my husband," she said with a false smile. "I, of all people, would know who Daniel is."

But instead of looking chagrined, Lloyd's expression turned darker. "If you are this man's wife, then there is no doubt in my mind that you know for certain that he is not Daniel Ropp. And to me, that makes you even worse, Sarah. You have taken in a man who is a liar. Who chose to adopt another man's life. I am almost more ashamed of you than him."

John raised his head. "That was uncalled for. You will apologize this minute."

Pandemonium rang out as everyone defended John and crowded around Sarah. Tears of relief fell down her cheeks as she realized that their secret wasn't going to be divulged. At least, not yet.

John took her arm and leaned close. "Let me take you home, Sarah."

Then Zeke carefully clapped his hands three times. Little by little, all talk quieted as he claimed their attention. "Lloyd, you sound mighty sure of yourself."

"I am."

"Then tell us, how do you know for sure that this man here ain't Daniel?"

"Besides the fact that I buried Daniel myself, I know because, like the rest of you, I've spent many an hour in Daniel's company. I've spent time with him, and I've seen him with his wife. And because of that I know without a doubt that I am right."

Jeremiah glared, obviously losing patience with all the grandstanding. "We do not need to sort this out now. It is not the right time or place."

Lloyd shook his head. "Of course this is the right time and place." Scanning the crowd, he said quietly, "Is there ever a wrong time to speak the truth . . . even if it isn't what we want to hear?"

As Lloyd's words echoed through the crowd, Sarah couldn't deny the truth in them.

She turned to John, met his gaze, then watched as he stepped away from her.

"Lloyd is right," John said. He swallowed hard, then pulled his shoulders back. "He was right about everything. As it says in Proverbs, 'Truthful words stand the test of time, but lies are soon exposed.'"

As Lloyd's eyes glittered with triumph, and everyone around her stared at John in confusion, Sarah realized that she'd only thought she'd experienced heartache before.

But nothing had ever been as painful as realizing that she was about to lose the one man she'd ever loved. The one man who had loved her back.

Eighteen

. . . .

Redemption

JOHN FIGURED THAT there was a time in each man's life when he was given more than he deserved. Perhaps a man was blessed with a good head on his shoulders; maybe it was a strong back. Other men he knew had been blessed with family that loved them unconditionally.

His blessing had been the gift of two precious months with Sarah.

For nearly the last thirty days, he'd lived in a real home and had been blessed to be in a real relationship. Still, it reflected sadly on his life that he'd had only thirty days to call truly special. It was true then, that those thirty days were more than he deserved.

But he was never a man to feel sorry for himself, or to fight the things that were painfully obvious.

Which meant that he was right to finally confess the truth. It was time to stop pretending his continued lies would somehow help Sarah, because nothing could help her now. He'd damaged her reputation beyond repair. He'd ruined her. And there was every reason to suppose that no one would ever believe her now. Or would ever hold her in esteem.

Clearing his throat, he stared at the men and women surrounding them. At everyone except Sarah. At this moment, he couldn't bear to meet her gaze. All it would do was make things harder.

"I am Jonathan Scott," he said simply. "And I came to Holmes County in order to claim property of Daniel Ropp's."

Though he didn't really feel the need to observe everyone's reaction to his confession, his gaze strayed toward Zeke. The younger man was glaring at him—and looking a bit full of himself, too. Almost as if he'd just been vindicated.

"You did more than that," Zeke said, unabashedly meeting John's gaze.

John shrugged. "You are right. I . . . I was even willing to pretend to be Daniel Ropp in order to get what I wanted."

Zeke glared. "And you brought Sarah into your dark scheme?"

"Not intentionally." After darting a quick look at Sarah, he amended his words. "I mean, not at first. At first, I lied to Sarah, too. I have no defense for myself."

Curious, stunned silence met his words.

Contempt filled Lloyd's expression. "You adopted another man's life. You lied to us all. You are truly an evil man."

John bent his head, ready to accept their disdain, but

to his surprise, Sarah stepped closer and came to his defense.

"He is not evil. I promise you all, he is not. You must give him a chance."

"A chance?" Lloyd raised his eyebrows at the crowd. "He has already had too many chances, I think."

The preacher raised his arm again, silencing them with one quick slash of his hand.

John braced himself for the worst. But instead, Jeremiah stared at John in such a way that it felt as if the holy man could look into his eyes and read his darkest, most private thoughts.

"Jonathan Scott, why would you do such a thing?" he inquired. "Why would you bring such grief and strife upon our community? Why would you dishonor a pure and moral widow like you did?"

John's heart felt like it had slowed to the speed of the slow, steady beat the drummer boys had tapped out on the battlefield.

Apprehension settled in. He knew his insides felt dire. He didn't want to lose Sarah. He didn't want to leave Holmes County. But more importantly, he didn't want Sarah to suffer if it was decided that he should be banished from their community.

He chose his words with care. "I know all of you might find this difficult to believe, but I promise that I never meant to betray all of you. I certainly never intended to hurt Sarah."

"Your words sound sincere, and I want to believe you.

But that does not negate the fact that you did those things anyway," Jeremiah pointed out. "It's time to explain yourself."

A hundred reasons filled his head. The money jar. The idea of being a landowner. Later, a home. Overriding everything was Sarah, and the way she'd changed his life, his whole outlook on his future.

But her impact was so personal, so meaningful to him, he didn't want to sully her name by connecting it with his. Not right at this moment. She was going to have enough pain without him making things worse. "I had my reasons. However, they are private."

"You are going to have to give us more explanation than that," Lloyd said.

John wasn't eager to share anything, but as he scanned the crowd, seeing the disbelief and hurt etched on everyone's faces, he knew that they did deserve something more than a terse statement.

Not daring to look at Sarah for fear that he would fall apart, he said, "I did meet Daniel in the war. I also fought by his side. When we weren't in battle, we spent time together sitting, sharing stories, talking—as soldiers often do." He looked at the men and women gathered, unable to keep a small smile from appearing. "For months, he talked about his home and his community. He talked about how much you all meant to him. When he died, I decided to do something I originally would have never imagined I was capable of doing. While I did that, I got to know Sarah."

Inwardly, he winced. Even to his ears his explanation sounded weak and reprehensible.

"That is your only explanation?" Zeke asked as the crowd grumbled.

"That is all I am willing to discuss, though I do have one last thing to say," he said, fearing that he might have already said too much publicly. "What I did, what I perpetrated on you all? It was unforgivable. I know this. To try to justify myself would be wrong. To ask your forgiveness would be shameful."

Pausing to take a breath, he glanced warily at Sarah.

She was still standing next to him, but her expression looked frozen, her eyes almost devoid of emotion. She looked like a paper replica of herself, so thin and weak. So frail, he feared she was on the verge of collapse.

Just then he noticed how the rest of the congregation seemed to be doing their best to pretend she didn't exist, or else were gazing at her with expressions of distaste.

Though he knew little about the Amish faith, he knew enough to realize that she was going to be cast out from her whole community. He could try to defend her, but it wouldn't do much good. His selfish reasons to obtain a fortune in all the wrong ways had obviously been unsuccessful.

And it didn't matter that it was unintentional. The damage had been done.

Zeke stepped forward, righteous anger evident in each step. "We offered your friendship. We welcomed you. You took a good man and ruined his memory. You have tainted us all with your sins and lies. You must leave."

John ached to say that Daniel Ropp had been a great many things, but he had certainly not been the good man

Zeke was making him out to be. He certainly hadn't been a caring husband to his honorable wife.

However, no matter how flawed Daniel had been, his sins paled when compared to John's. "I will leave you all at the earliest opportunity," he said quietly. "You will never see me again."

"As if that would help your soul. As if that would help anything." Zeke sneered. "You ruined Sarah."

John flinched and turned to Sarah, looking for a sign. Looking for anything to give him hope. But instead, she remained motionless. Frozen and strong. Didn't so much as flinch.

And then he realized what Zeke's true meaning had been. He wasn't thinking simply of Sarah caring for or taking in a man like him. No, they were thinking of something far darker.

Their condemnation was so disquieting, her hurt was so heartbreaking, and his feelings so strong, he lashed out. "I did not ruin Sarah. I've barely touched her," he blurted before he could remind himself that he'd sworn to keep her name off his tongue. "But in many ways, you all did. You blamed her for her husband's cruelty and headstrong ways. You ignored her when she was all alone, choosing instead of focus on your own needs."

"That isn't true," Zeke said. "We all looked out for her."

"You gave her charity. You gave her what you could, hoping to feel good about yourselves, but you didn't offer her what she needed the most . . . your friendship."

"I wouldn't be so quick to cast stones," one of the women

in the crowd said. "It would seem to me that you have plenty of sins to pay for."

"I do. And I know for the rest of my life I will rue the day I neglected to see the right path for myself, concentrating on how desolate my life felt instead. I should have kept my faith."

"We have no need to hear any more words about your faults and failures," Lloyd said. "It don't serve no purpose, except to remind us all of how you lied and knowingly set to fool us."

Of course, that was not what he'd set out to do. All he'd really wanted was to take some money no one else knew existed and create a life for himself. It was only after experiencing Sarah's kindness and love that his intentions got waylaid.

Lloyd's glare burned. "What we should do is string you up to the nearest tree." His face flushed as he shook a fist in the air. "That is what your kind would do, you know. And for once? Why, I agree with it. You deserve nothing. You have put the whole community in jeopardy."

Zeke stepped forward, his eyes glittering with anger. "Jonathan Scott is the very worst sort of man. He duped all of us. No doubt he spent many an evening laughing at our gullibility. Sarah, too."

"No," John blurted.

Zeke raised his brows. "No, what? No you didn't laugh at us? No, Sarah didn't join you?"

"No, you shouldn't bring her into my misdeeds."

Looking pained, Jeremiah clapped his hands twice. When Lloyd, Zeke, and John turned to him, he shook his head in dismay. "I will have no more talk like that, especially from you, Lloyd and Zeke."

Zeke puffed out his chest. "Me?"

The formidable preacher's gray eyebrows snapped together. "You, son, are letting your tongue wag your brain. I am sure when you lift your head and clear your hurts you will realize that you are saying words you do not mean." With a small grunt of impatience, he turned to Lloyd. "And you, Lloyd, need to rethink your anger. Though you have just returned from battle, I must say that I am surprised at the way that you rushed to cast stones."

Lloyd and Zeke looked away but didn't apologize.

With a sigh, the preacher pushed his way through the circle of men to stand in front of Sarah. "Sarah, what do you have to say about all this?"

It hurt to see her questioned publicly. For most of her life, she'd suffered in silence. Made do with less. Expected nothing from her neighbors and been offered nothing.

Unable to stop himself, he wrapped an arm around her shoulders. He needed to touch her in some way so she knew that she wasn't alone. Her muscles eased under his hand, making him realize that she'd truly thought he would let her stand alone in front of the crowd.

"She had nothing to do with my transgressions," he blurted. "Sarah is blameless. An innocent."

Sarah still stood stoically, but he felt a small tremor pass through her like a sigh.

John hoped his words would deflect any further focus on Sarah, but Jeremiah had other plans.

Looking aggrieved by John's interruption, he said, "Jonathan Scott, you have had your opportunity to speak. So has Lloyd. Both of you, along with Ezekiel here, are talking about what Sarah did or didn't do. But that ain't enough. I, for one, would like to hear what she has to say."

Feeling like his heart was breaking, John met her gaze. In that one second, it felt as if a thousand thoughts and yearnings were being exchanged.

Still eager to protect her—even though this whole mess was his fault—he drew a breath. He was ready to remind her that she didn't need to say anything at all. But she held up a hand.

"I need to do this, John," she said quietly before facing the preacher. "Jeremiah, it is true that at first I was fooled. For a long time I thought he was Daniel, returned from the war. I was relieved he was back, glad he had not died."

It was obvious that she was choosing each word with care, weighing it in her mind before sharing. After a brief pause, she visibly steeled herself and spoke again. "But then I began to suspect this man was not the Daniel I had known. Actually, though I tried hard to ignore what my eyes and ears saw, I was fairly sure he was not my husband."

With a shy smile his way, she shook her head. "This man, he was too different. Actually, I have a feeling that my heart knew he was not Daniel way before my brain accepted that."

"But yet you didn't say anything to the rest of us." Zeke glared. "Why on earth not? I, I mean, we could have saved you."

"But I didn't need saving."

"Of course—"

"Let her speak, Ezekiel," Jeremiah interrupted. His tone was so stern, his piercing glare so adamant, no man would have ignored him.

John stood helplessly as he watched Sarah—his wife—gather her strength. After the briefest of hesitations, she pulled her shoulders back, lifted her chin, and raised her voice. Almost as if she was daring one and all to disregard her words.

"Zeke, I didn't need saving because part of me liked this new man." With yet another small smile at him, she added, "John, here, was an answer to my prayers."

Several people frowned at her. Some even eyed her with disapproval. But Sarah didn't seem bothered any longer.

"The truth of the matter is that I began to suspect John was not Daniel when he didn't slap me across the face or jerk my arm when I didn't follow his bidding right away," she said, her voice strong and sure. "I began to doubt he was my husband when he didn't yell at me for the hens laying only two eggs instead of three. Or when I spilled the water I'd heated for his bath."

John ached for Sarah as she folded her arms around her waist. She was so obviously striving for control.

"That had been what I was used to, you see."

Dismay filled the crowd, along with a few shaking heads.

But John also noticed that no one acted terribly surprised. No, from what he could discern, they seemed only stunned that she would admit such things.

Every fiber of his being wanted to step in, to tell her that she didn't need to defend herself or him any longer. But by now he knew her well enough to realize that she needed to tell everyone her story. She needed it as much as he'd needed to believe that there was something more to life than pain and heartache.

When she regained her composure, Sarah continued. "I lived with Daniel for a year and a half and suffered under his hand. I lived with his arrogance, with his changeable moods and his unhappiness. But most of all, I lived with his anger. It never seemed to disappear. If anything, he became more impatient, more harsh." Her voice began to crack. "My life with him? Well, it was mighty hard." After taking a cleansing breath, she added, "It was also hard to see how everyone pitied me—but never tried to intervene."

"He was your husband," Ana, Zeke's sister pointed out. "There was nothing we could say or do. It wouldn't have been right."

"I agree," Sarah said quietly. "I knew I was alone, and that I spoke solemn vows saying that I would obey my husband and honor him. But I would also be lying if I didn't sometimes wish that someone else would offer to help me. I was at his mercy, Ana."

John felt his throat burn with heavy emotion. It was hard to watch this gentle woman reveal just how difficult and painful her life had been.

Sarah continued. "When Daniel left to go join the regiment in Pennsylvania, I have to admit that I was relieved. I knew he was mighty unhappy, and I hoped and prayed that his going to battle would change him. Give him something that our quiet life here in Holmes County had not."

Sarah looked around at the faces of everyone again. "When we all saw his name on the list of casualties, I was just as shocked and dismayed as any of you. He'd been such a large presence in my life, I couldn't imagine the war injuring or killing him." She sighed. "Of course I prayed for his soul. Of course I grieved for him. But I wasn't mourning for the man he was, I was mourning the man he could have been."

After taking a breath, she gestured to John. "But when this man came into my life, he made me believe in hope again."

She glanced his way, and happiness lit her eyes as well as her lips. "When I realized John had taken Daniel's identity, I felt betrayed, too. No one wants to be lied to. And I didn't understand why he would do such a thing, either. But if you want to truly know why I didn't ask him to leave? It is because I knew what married life was like, living with a man I didn't love. I also knew what it was like to live completely alone. To be scared when snowstorms and thunderstorms came. To be exhausted in the hot summer heat. To know that no matter how much I hoped and prayed, no one was likely to come to my assistance."

"I came by," Zeke said.

"Yes, you did. And I was grateful for your concern. But I'm afraid I yearned for something more."

John watched Zeke flush as her words and their meaning sank in. Then he turned as Sarah continued.

"But until Jonathan Scott arrived, I'd had no knowledge of what a good marriage could be like. I hadn't realized that it was still possible for me to be happy."

"But you couldn't possibly have been happy. Why, everything you'd been doing was against the Lord's will! You chose to live in sin and lie to your friends and church," Lloyd said. "Sarah, it pains me to say this, but you've twisted the truth in order to live with yourself."

"Maybe I have twisted things a bit," she allowed. "But a part of me figured that the Lord had a whole lot to do with John appearing on our land. I don't believe in coincidence." Looking into the crowd, she added, "Surely only the Lord could have brought about the friendship of two such different men? One was English, one was Amish, and yet they looked so much alike. Furthermore, they met in the middle of a war—and Daniel trusted him enough to tell him his secrets."

Jeremiah gazed at her seriously. "Put that way, it does seem like the Lord had a lot to do with John appearing in our midst."

Zeke crossed his arms on top of his chest. "But that doesn't change how you pretended to be his wife."

Just as John was about to announce yet again that he'd never touched Sarah, hadn't ever done anything more than hold her hand briefly, Sarah spoke.

"Zeke, when I discovered who Jonathan was, after I forgave him, I agreed to marry him."

While the rest of the crowd gasped, Jeremiah's eyes narrowed. "What are you saying, Sarah?"

"Two weeks ago, I rode by Jonathan's side to Mansfield and married him in a courthouse. We are guilty of many things. But not of living in sin. We are legally wed."

Zeke's eyes were wide and his cheeks were flushed. "Sarah, you married an Englischer? In an English courthouse?"

Her chin lifted. "I did."

As John expected, there were no smiles of congratulations or offerings of best wishes. Instead there was an almost tangible separation from her by the congregation.

Except by their esteemed preacher. He turned to John. "Why did you marry her, John? Why did you exchange vows? You could have never done so, choosing to shame her. You could have simply left."

It was never so easy to speak from his heart. "I had no intention of shaming her. She is the most virtuous woman I've ever met."

But Jeremiah continued to press. "Why, then? Was it because you wanted to continue in Daniel's place?"

"I wanted to continue in Daniel's place, that is true. But it wasn't because I wanted to have land or live in a home of my own. It was because of Sarah." Pulling his shoulders back, John slowly scanned the thirty or so people surrounding them.

Dared to meet their eyes.

Then he raised his voice so that there would be no chance for anyone to misunderstand what he was saying. "I married Sarah Ropp for one reason only: because I'd fallen in love with her. I wanted to have her as my wife." Gathering his courage, he gazed at her.

And then it truly felt like they were the only two people in the Millers' yard.

"Sarah, though our marriage wasn't blessed in a church, I meant every word of my vows. I will always love and cherish you. I always intend to honor and hold you. No matter what happens, where I go, what you do, in my heart, you will always be my wife."

Tears filled her eyes. Her bottom lip trembled.

More than anything, John yearned to take her into his arms and comfort her. Hold her tightly, kiss her brow, and say all the words that had been held so tightly in his heart.

But it wasn't quite that time.

John continued. "She and I decided to keep my real identity a secret because I feared what would happen to her if everyone learned the truth. It wasn't easy. I knew Daniel. Not as well as the rest of you, but I knew him on the battlefield. I spent hours by his side, listening to his views on everything from farming to his faith to the way he chose to treat his wife. I won't deny his bravery, but I must admit that I had no desire to 'be' him. I didn't respect his opinions on a lot of things."

A few men murmured to each other. And John saw Lloyd look at him in a new way. Though it wasn't going to change a thing about his future, he was glad of that. Ready to be done with all the explanations, ready to pull Sarah away from the many sets of peering eyes, he murmured, "In the end I was willing to be a man I didn't like very much in order to save Sarah's reputation. Obviously, even that plan was wrong."

"Oh, John," Sarah murmured.

After spying the tears that were now running down his

wife's cheeks, he nodded his head to Jeremiah. "Thank you for allowing me to say my piece. And though it might not mean much, I am very sorry for any distress or hurt I have caused. That was never my intention."

Figuring that this would be the very last time he would be in their midst, he said, "I am an unworthy man. I know it, and I don't dispute it. But for a little bit of time, I got to be someone else. I began to imagine that I was worthy of a good woman's love. I got to feel what it was like to have a place in a real community. For once in my life, I wasn't alone." He tipped his hat. "And for that, I want to thank you all."

Then, before the crowd could call out more questions or subject Sarah to any more painful revelations, he leaned close to his wife. "This has gone on long enough," he whispered. "We don't owe anyone another word of explanation." As she stood there, silently staring up at him in wonder, he wrapped a secure arm around her shoulders. "Let me get you on home now, Sarah."

But instead of immediately following his lead, she shrugged off his arm. "Did you mean it?" she asked, pure wonder lacing her voice. "Do you love me? Truly?"

Though others could hear them—why, some were even shamelessly eavesdropping!—he spoke the words she longed to hear. Proving that he could deny her nothing. "I love you more than you could ever imagine, Sarah. I love you more than I have words to say."

Her blue eyes turned languid. Trust and something he wasn't brave enough to name entered her gaze.

Then, at last, she let him guide her away.

Slowly, side by side, they walked. Away from the crowd surrounding the barn. Away from Lloyd and Zeke and the dozens of other people with questions and jibes and hurts.

Each step felt like it was taking them miles away, but of course that was figuratively. Instead, she was walking by his side, one small step at a time. Making slow progress, but also taking great strides from everything she'd ever known.

John felt her pain, worried over her impending isolation. Indeed, he had a very good feeling that she might not ever feel welcome in their midst again. And because he was subjecting her to yet another life of loneliness, John knew he'd never felt more undeserving.

But still, what was done was done. There was no denying that. And no denying that he had to put his trust and faith in the Lord. Because just as he believed that the Lord had brought them together, he knew that He must have also brought Lloyd Mast into their midst for a very good reason.

John just wished he didn't hurt so much.

There seemed nothing to say anymore. Without talking, they got into the wagon and gently nudged the horse forward. Off the Millers' land and down a vacant road. As the horse trotted along the dirt road, acting as if she was pleased to be free, John searched his mind for a way to make things better for her.

But of course he could not.

He'd ruined her life in multiple ways. And he'd already surpassed any chance for redemption.

"John?" she asked after they'd gone almost a mile.

"Yes?" he asked, bracing himself to hear her complaints. To hear her crying.

"*Ich liebe dich.* I love you."

He jerked on the reins so hard the horse protested. "What did you say?" he asked.

"You heard me. I know that. And," she added in a low voice, "I think you know what my words meant." She laughed then, and the sound was light and lovely in the cool evening air. Lightening his spirit in a way he'd never imagined could happen.

He turned his head and glanced at her. Then, not trusting his eyes, glanced at her again.

But what he saw was so beautiful and true, a shudder surged through him. So strong and violent, coming as such a surprise—it almost made him stop the wagon.

Her words were more precious than he ever imagined. Her laughter, her happiness? Why, it was more than he'd ever dreamt.

So very much more.

After they'd gone another hundred feet or so, Sarah reached out and carefully squeezed his arm. "John? Don't you have anything to say? I, ah, thought you would have a response for me."

Glad that they were now only yards from their farm's entrance, John veered the wagon onto their land and finally halted the horse.

And then, he did what he'd been wanting to do from the moment he first saw her blue eyes. He pulled her into his arms, held her close, and kissed her with everything he had.

She stilled. For a moment, he thought he'd frightened her. But then she melted in his arms and raised hers, finally encircling him, caressing his scarred neck, his skin. Offering up her lips to his.

And it was everything he'd ever dreamt of.

She had accepted him. His sad past. His lack of funds. His scarred body. His faults.

She'd accepted all of his sins. All of him, and had given him the most miraculous gift in the world—acceptance and love. Love for what he was, not for who he could have been or who he should have been.

Love for who he was right here and right now.

And that gift was more precious than diamonds or dreams. It was everything.

Feeling overwhelmed, he pulled away and pressed his lips to her forehead.

She looked at him curiously. "Is something wrong?"

"Not at all." This time, he felt like he should be the one laughing. "Nothing at all."

Her expression gentling, she reached up and ran her hand along his cheek. The scarred one again. "Aren't you going to say anything about what I said?"

"About you loving me?"

Her other hand reached up and brushed his other cheek. Holding his face in between her hands. "Well, yes."

"I would love to say something, Sarah. Something right and perfect and lovely. But at this very moment? Truly, I am speechless."

She smiled, then.

And he knew he'd come home.

He'd come home at last.

Epilogue

·········

One Month Later

AT SARAH'S URGING, they'd decided to walk to the gathering at the Yoders' house. The invitation to join in the celebration for the family's newborn daughter had come as something of a surprise, and for several hours after Kristie Yoder had stopped by to deliver the invitation, Sarah had fretted something fierce.

John had let her fret and stew for a spell, knowing that she sometimes needed that. Then, after listening to her worry for almost an hour, he'd taken control. "I think we should go," he'd said.

"But what if everyone scorns us? That would ruin Kristie's day."

"I reckon she's already considered that," he said lightly. "After all, she was the one who delivered the invitation. Let's go," he whispered, pressing his lips to her brow. "It's time."

"We might merely be ignored," she said.

He'd smiled at the hope in her voice. "Ignored is better than being completely shunned, I suppose."

And though they'd kept to themselves during the last month, they hadn't been sent from the community. John had been surprised. He'd imagined that their retribution would be a bit harsher. Even though he knew the Amish were peaceful people, John hadn't truly believed that the community would ever find it easy to accept him or forgive his misdeeds.

But to his surprise, the preacher Jeremiah had arrived just a week after Lloyd's return and John's confession. Sarah had been so pleased to see him but afraid, too.

But Jeremiah was a true man of God. He'd merely accepted Sarah's offer of coffee—declining her offer of milk and sugar with a smile—and then had settled down for a long talk with both of them.

It seemed that John's speech about his love for Sarah had resonated with all of them.

And that speech, together with everyone's knowledge that Sarah had lived a mighty difficult life with her first husband, had encouraged many in the community to reach out to them.

Oh, of course John and Sarah were not Amish anymore. And they might never have the close bond with their neighbors and friends that they might have had in other circumstances . . . but Jeremiah had been forceful in reminding them that they still had a place in the community. They were still wanted.

If they wanted to be.

After Jeremiah left, the two of them weighed the preacher's words. Soon, it was very clear that Sarah wanted to be accepted more than anything.

Secretly, John yearned for the same things. But he'd learned the hard way that wanting something—especially wanting other people's friendship and love—didn't necessarily mean that such wishes could be granted. Now, here they were, going to the Yoders. And since John still found it difficult to drive a buggy, they'd elected to walk. Besides, now that he was no longer pretending to be someone he wasn't, he figured it was time to let everyone else get used to the fact that he was an Englischer, too.

Sarah was walking straight and proud by his side.

Now she wore a gold ring on her finger, and he couldn't deny the pride he felt every time he saw the simple gold band on her left hand. She was wonderful and she, by the grace of God, was his, and he was so happy to let everyone know it.

She'd come so far since they'd first met and he was so proud of her. For so long she'd been everything and yet almost nothing to the people in her community. It had been a hard road for her to take, and John felt that a lesser woman would have broken down under the stress of it all.

But not his Sarah. After they'd finally admitted everything to the community, his wife had become her own person. Slowly and surely she was holding her head a little higher and being a little more confident.

She was no longer wearing her *kapp*, but was wearing a smaller head covering that some of the Mennonite women in the area wore. Her dress was a light blue, too, and had a little collar on it. And there were also buttons.

It was a far cry from what the English women in town wore, but it was also a step away from dressing Amish.

He knew in his heart that if Daniel had survived she would have stayed by his side and tried every day to make things work. And if he had never come to the area, John was pretty sure that she would have married Zeke and lived a good and happy life as his Amish wife.

Instead, she'd been willing to give up much of herself for a man like him. A scarred, almost ruined man whose only real claim of worth was that he loved her.

He thought she'd never been more beautiful.

"Are you nervous about seeing everyone?" he asked as they walked on the small bridge over Sugar Creek. Now they were mere minutes from the Yoder farm.

"*Jah.*" She shrugged. "I can't help it. I am asking a lot of them, letting me still be a part of the community sometimes."

"Don't forget, they asked you to come to the party. I think that says a lot about how far they've come."

"I haven't forgotten that they asked us, John," she murmured softly. "They asked both of us." With a small, gentle smile, she added, "See, they want to know you, too."

"I still can't believe that. It's more than I expected."

"The Amish are more than many expect, I think."

He liked the way that sounded, almost as much as he liked the way she sounded. So sure of herself. Confident. Perky.

"Don't forget, if someone is mean to you, I want you to tell me immediately." He still didn't trust Zeke to behave himself, though Sarah had said she had no worries in that regard. But what she didn't seem to realize was that Zeke's hurt and anger had less to do with John pretending to be someone he wasn't and more to do with Zeke nursing a broken heart.

"What are you going to do, John? Give them what-for?" she teased.

He chuckled, liking the sound of his favorite phrase on her lips. "Maybe."

"I don't think anyone will be rude. They promised to accept us, after all."

"I hope that's the case." He paused, remembering what Lloyd had told him the evening before when he'd stopped by. "Lloyd said it would be."

She shook her head in wonder. "I still can't believe that you and he have become such fast friends. When he exposed you for not being Daniel, I was sure you would always be enemies."

"I thought so, too. No one was more surprised to see him at our front door than I." Reflecting on that, he added, "Sarah, I think we get along because we both survived the war. It's nice to have someone nearby who understands what it was like."

She squeezed his arm, telling him without words that she understood the harsh memories and pain he still fought in the middle of the night.

Just that one touch gave him strength. He cleared his throat. "But if Lloyd had never wanted to talk to me again, I wouldn't have blamed him, if you want to know the truth. Lloyd Mast is an upstanding man. It was his right to be disdainful of a man who was willing to take another's identity."

"*Jah*, he is upstanding. But he is not perfect, John. Nor does he wish to be. Only the Lord is."

"He told me much the same thing. I have a lot to learn about forgiveness."

"We all do. But it is not our right to punish. That is the Lord's place."

"I hear you, Sarah. And I promise, I am trying hard to believe that."

"And that you are worthy of such love and forgiveness?"

In truth, that was a far harder thing for him to swallow. But he was doing his best to accept such things. "I'm trying my best. I want to believe."

She smiled. "Then that is enough, John."

"I hope so."

"I promise, it is."

But then when they walked over the rise, she paused and he saw a small tremor pass through her body. "Look at all the buggies and people at the Yoders! Oh, my goodness, John! When Kristie came over to invite us, I had envisioned it to be a much smaller gathering."

"I know you did."

"I want to be strong, but I am a little afraid." To his surprise, she raised her left hand and gazed at the gold band encircling her finger.

It practically killed him to say it, but he didn't want to ever cause her a moment's pain. "Would you like to take off your ring during the party?"

She whipped her head to his. "No! Why would you ask such a thing?"

"I saw you look at your hand. And seeing as how the Amish don't wear wedding rings, I thought maybe you would feel too conspicuous."

"Oh, I was only thinking that I like wearing your ring.

It helps me remember that I am no longer alone. I know the Lord is always with me. But the ring reminds me that I am no longer alone in my heart."

Now those were words to treasure. John exhaled, and stood quietly by her side, telling her without words that he would follow her lead. Let her take as much time as she needed to get ready to join the crowd.

After a minute, because there was no one else there to see, he wrapped a reassuring arm around her shoulders. "It looks like it will be a wonderful gathering. I'm sure you will be most welcome."

"I hope so."

Dropping his hand, he said, "Are you ready to go to the party, Sarah?"

"I am." She started forward, her expression serious.

He knew that look; it was one she'd worn around him when he'd first arrived. Now he knew she wore it like a mask, as a way of protecting herself from pain.

As they got closer to the groups of people, first a couple of heads rose. Then, like a wave on an ocean, almost everyone stopped and stared.

And then, a few women stepped forward. As did Lloyd.

"It's about time you two got here," Lloyd called out with a cheeky grin. "What did you do, stop every five minutes and make a wish? Rest?"

"We decided to walk," John said easily. "It took a bit longer than we anticipated."

Then he glanced Sarah's way. Just in time to see her being gathered into the women's group. And to his amusement, the other women were holding on to her hand and exclaiming over her band of gold.

He heard her laugh. Then saw her look his way and smile. That smile was bright and genuine and perfect.

And that was when he realized everything Jeremiah and Sarah, and even Daniel, had tried to teach him.

Though they weren't perfect, though they all made mistakes, though they all sinned . . . they were all worthy. Even the smallest mustard seed.

Even him.

Author's Note

· · · · · · · · · · ·

Dear Readers,

It's funny how some stories come to pass. Several years
ago, I came across an article written by a history scholar de-
scribing how the Amish in Holmes County dealt with the
Civil War. Some did their best to ignore the war completely.
Others paid fees to the Union in exchange for not fighting.
But there was one small group of Anabaptists who elected to
send seven men to join the cause. They were very opposed to
slavery and wanted to do something to show their support.

Now there was a story!

I took that small bit of truth and let my imagination take
over. I started imagining what life would have been like for
the women who were left behind. I also wondered what it
must have been like for the men to return home again. Then
I decided to shake things up a bit and created a damaged hero
who was searching for redemption and love . . . and who also
happened to have a very big secret.

And that is how I came to write *Redemption*. It's romantic and a bit far-fetched . . . but sometimes it's fun to let one's imagination take flight. I truly enjoyed writing it. I hope you enjoyed it, too.

With my best,
Shelley Shepard Gray

Eager for more heartfelt romance
from Shelley Shepard Gray?

Keep reading for an excerpt from the first book
in Shelley's new series, Return to Sugarcreek

HOPEFUL

Now available from Avon Inspire

One

. . . .

September

SHE WAS LATE.

Holding her canvas tote bag in one hand and a box of oatmeal-raisin cookies in the other, Miriam Zehr exited her house, darted down her street, turned left on Main Street, and almost ran down old Mr. Sommers.

With a grunt, he stepped to the side, his garden hose spraying a good bit of water onto her skirts before settling back onto his daffodils.

She skidded to a stop. "I'm sorry, Eli."

He merely raised one eyebrow. "Late again, Miriam?"

"*Jah.*" As discreetly as possible, she shook her blue apron and dress a bit. A few drops flew from the fabric, glinting in the morning sun.

He shook his head in exasperation. "One day you're going to injure someone with your haste."

She winced. "I know. And I am sorry, Eli."

Looking at the box in her hand, his voice turned wheedling. "Those cookies?"

"They're oatmeal-raisin." When his eyes brightened, she set down her tote and carefully opened the box. "Care for one?"

After setting the hose down, he reached in and pulled out two plump cookies. "Girl who cooks as *gut* as you should be married by now."

She'd heard the same refrain almost as often as she'd run late for work. "I've often thought the same thing," she said as she picked up her tote again. "But for now, I must be on my way."

"Have a care, now." He shook one arthritic finger at her. "Not everyone's as spry as me, you know."

"I'll be careful," she promised before continuing on her way to work.

Once at the Sugarcreek Inn, she would put on a crisp white apron. Then, she'd divide her time between baking pies and serving the restaurant's guests. The whole time, she'd do her best to smile brightly. Chat with customers and her co-workers. And pretend she didn't yearn for a different life.

But first, she had to get to work on time.

"Going pretty fast today, Miriam," Joshua Graber called out from the front porch of his family's store. "How late are you?"

"Only five minutes. Hopefully."

He laughed. "Good luck. Stop by soon, wouldja? Gretta would love to see you."

"I'll do my best."

Now that the Inn was finally in view, she slowed her pace and began to stroll to the restaurant, trying to catch her breath.

As she got closer, she forced herself to look at the building with a critical eye. There were places where it needed some touching up. A fresh coat of paint. One of the windowsills needed to be replaced.

The landscaping around the front door was a little shaggy, a little overgrown. It needed a bit of sprucing up, a little bit of tender loving care.

Kind of like herself, she supposed. Now that she was twenty-five, she was tired of biding her time, waiting in vain for something new to happen.

Perhaps it really was time to think about doing something different. Going somewhere new. For too long now she'd been everyone's helper and assistant. She'd watched her best friends be courted, fall in love, and get married. Most were expecting their first babies. Some, like Josh and Gretta, already had two children.

Yes, it seemed like everyone had moved forward in their lives except for her.

The sad thing was that there was no need to stay in Sugarcreek any longer. She had plenty of money saved and even her parents' blessing to go find her happiness.

So why hadn't she done anything yet? Was she afraid . . . or still holding out hope that a certain man would finally notice her and see that she was the perfect girl for him?

That she'd actually been the perfect one for years now?

Pushing aside that disturbing thought, she slipped inside the Sugarcreek Inn and prepared to offer her excuses to Jana Kent, the proprietor.

Her boss was standing by a pair of bookshelves, unboxing more of the knickknacks she'd recently started selling in an attempt to drum up a bit more business and profit for the inn.

Jana paused when she walked by. "Cutting it close today, Miriam."

Glancing up at the clock over the door, Miriam winced. It was ten after nine. Jana had long since given up on Miriam getting to work early or even on time. Now she merely hoped Miriam wouldn't be too late. "I know. Sorry."

"What's today's excuse?" Humor lit Jana's eyes, telling Miriam that while she might feel exasperated, she wasn't mad.

Usually, Miriam came up with an amusing story or fib. Over the years, earthquakes had erupted, washing machines had overflowed, ravenous dogs had invaded her yard.

Today, however, her mind drew a complete blank. "Time simply got away from me this morning."

Jana looked almost disappointed. "That's it?"

Miriam shrugged weakly. "I'll come up with a better excuse tomorrow, I'm sure of it."

"Miriam Zehr. You are one of my best employees and one of my hardest workers. You always offer to help other people, and you never mind staying late. Why is it so hard for you to get here on time?"

There were all kinds of reasons. Miriam wasn't a morning person. She seemed to always sleep in. She hated to get to work early so she waited until the last second to leave her house.

Unfortunately, though, she feared it was her somewhat irrational way of rebelling against the continual routine of her life. Sometimes her frenetic morning journey to work was the biggest excitement of her day.

Inching away, she mumbled, "I'll go put on my apron and get to work."

"Thank you, Miriam."

Hurrying toward the back, Miriam scanned the tables. Quite a few were empty.

And then she noticed He was there. Junior Beiler. All six-foot-two inches of brawn. Blond hair and perfection.

Junior, the object of too many of her daydreams. The boy she'd had a crush on for as long as she could remember. The man she yearned would truly notice her.

Miriam kept walking, trying not to look his way. Trying not to stare. But she did. And as she did, she noticed that he was staring right back at her. More important, she was sure that something like interest glinted in his blue eyes.

Feeling her cheeks flush, she darted into the kitchen. But the moment the doors closed behind her, she let herself smile.

Maybe today, at long last, would be different.

THE MOMENT JUNIOR Beiler saw the kitchen doors swing shut, he grinned at Joe. "You were right, Miriam Zehr works here. I just saw her walk by."

Joe's expression turned smug. "I told you she did."

"She just went into the kitchens." Drumming his fingers on the table, he murmured, "I hope she comes out again soon."

Joe chuckled. "And when she does? Are you actually going to talk to her about what's been on your mind?"

"Absolutely." Noticing that his buddy's expression looked skeptical, he straightened his shoulders a bit. "What's wrong with that?"

"Just about everything. You can't simply go asking women about their best friends and expect to get information. It ain't done, ya know."

"Why not?" It made perfect sense to him.

"A woman isn't going to give you information if she doesn't know you."

Junior scoffed. As usual, Joe was making a big deal over nothing. "I've known Miriam for years. We both have, Joe."

"*Jah*, we went to *shool* with her, that's true. And we're all in the same church district. But let me ask you this, when was the last time you actually talked to her?"

"I'm pretty sure I said hello to her at church last Sunday."

Joe tilted his head slightly. "Did you? Or did you walk right by like you usually do?"

For the first time, Junior felt vaguely uncomfortable. He was one of eight kids, and he was sandwiched between two girls in his family. Because of that, he'd learned a thing or two about the female mind over the years. "I might have only thought about saying hello," he said grudgingly.

Joe looked triumphant. "See?"

Okay, Joe probably had a point. But his inattentiveness didn't mean he didn't like Miriam. He just had never thought about her much.

Until he realized she'd recently become good friends with Mary Kate Hershberger. Beautiful Mary Kate Hershberger, who had moved to Sugarcreek in August and had quickly caught his unwavering attention.

Joe grabbed another hot biscuit from the basket on the table and began slathering it with peanut butter spread. "I still think you should get your sister Kaylene to introduce you. After all, Mary Kate is Kaylene's teacher."

"*Nee*. Kaylene is having trouble in school." Lowering his voice, he said, "Actually, I'm not certain Kaylene is all that fond of her new teacher."

"Don't see why that matters."

"It does." His youngest sister was eight years old and the apple of his eye. There was no way he was going to use little Kaylene in order to get a date.

"Why?"

Luckily, the kitchen doors swung open again, and out came Miriam. She now had on a white apron over her dress, and was holding a coffeepot in her right hand. Seizing his chance, he turned his coffee cup right side up, waited until she was looking his way, and motioned her over.

Joe raised his brows. "Impressive," he muttered.

When she got to their table, her cheeks were flushed. "*Kaffi?*"

"*Jah*. For both of us."

After she'd filled both their cups, Joe gave him a little kick.

Thinking quickly, Junior asked, "So, Miriam, how have you been?"

She looked a bit startled by the question. "Me? I've been *gut*. Why do you ask?"

"No reason. It's just that, well . . . I mean, I haven't seen you around lately."

She looked at him curiously. "Where have you been looking?"

"Nowhere. I mean, I guess I haven't seen you anywhere but at *gmay*, at church. And here," he added, feeling like a fool.

Joe groaned as he took another bite of biscuit.

"Why were you looking? Did you need something?" Miriam asked.

His tongue was starting to feel like it was too big for his mouth. "Actually, ah . . . yes!" Seizing the opportunity, he added, "I've been wantin' to talk to you about something."

She set the coffeepot right on the table. "You have?"

"Yes. When do you get off work? Can I stop by?"

"You want to come by my house? Tonight?" Her cheeks pinkened.

"I do. May I come over?"

"You may . . . if you'd like. I'll be off work at four."

"*Gut*. I'll stop over around six."

"Do you need my address?"

"No, I know where you live. I'll see you then."

Miriam picked up the coffeepot, smiled shyly, then walked on.

When they were alone again, Junior picked up his coffee cup and took a fortifying sip. "See, Joe? That wasn't so hard."

"It wasn't so *gut*."

"Really?"

Joe leaned back in his chair and folded his arms across his chest. "You, Junior, are an idiot."

"What are you talking about? I'm going to go over to Miriam's house tonight and talk to her about Mary Kate. It's a *gut* plan. *Wunderbaar*."

After making sure Miriam wasn't nearby to overhear, Joe hissed, "Miriam doesna think you're coming over to ask about Mary Kate. She thinks you're going courting. How do you think she's going to feel when she discovers that you only want her help to get Mary Kate's attention?"

For the first time, Junior was starting to realize that he should have thought things through a bit more. "Oh. Well, I didn't think of that. I guess . . . the way I asked . . . It's not going to go well, is it?"

"Nope. You've truly made a mess of it. This is not good, Junior."

Warily, Junior glanced in the direction Joe was looking. Spied Miriam.

Noticed that she was standing near the hostess station. Her light blue eyes were bright with happiness. She was smiling softly.

Meeting her gaze, he felt his neck flush.

He had a sudden feeling that Joe was right. And that was not good.

Definitely not good at all.

Two

· · · · · · · · · ·

THIS HAD TO be the best day of her entire life.

After twenty-five years of hoping and praying for a change, of doing her best to be happy for her girlfriends when they'd fallen in love, after trying diets and hair tonics unsuccessfully to try to improve her looks, it had happened.

The boy she'd always wanted had finally looked her way.

God had finally answered her prayers! *"Danke,* Got," she whispered. For a moment, she considered reminding Him that she probably hadn't needed to wait quite so long for His blessings . . . but she decided against that.

After all, anyone who was anyone knew that the Lord worked in mysterious ways.

Standing behind one of the stainless steel counters in the kitchen, Miriam couldn't stop smiling. She wasn't sure what she'd done to finally attract the attention of Junior Beiler, but she wasn't about to question her good fortune. After years of looking at him longingly, he'd finally looked back.

And now he was coming to call that very evening!

Across the vast commercial kitchen, her three coworkers kept glancing at her curiously. Finally, Marla spoke. "I've never seen you so happy to roll out piecrust. Why are you in such a *wonderful-gut* mood?"

Miriam was tempted to share her news. Marla was a good friend, just a few years older than herself, and recently married. Miriam knew that she'd relish hearing about a new romance. But even more tempting was the chance to hold Junior's sudden interest close to her heart.

After all, there would be plenty of time for everyone to comment about their relationship when he took her out walking or for a buggy ride.

"I'm *frayt* today, that's all," she said airily.

Marla exchanged glances with Ruth and Christina. "Do you believe that our Miriam is simply happy, girls?"

"Not even for a minute," Ruth answered, even though, at fifty, she was far from a girl. Ruth had been married, widowed, and now worked at the Sugarcreek Inn beside them in a way that made Miriam forget that she hadn't always been there. And even though Ruth was English and favored faded jeans and T-shirts instead of dresses, aprons, and *kapps*, she was definitely one of their gang. "Come on, Miriam, give us a hint. Jana is in quite the mood today. Every time she comes in here, she fusses. Tell us something good."

Miriam grabbed a handful of flour and took her time spreading it on the counter. "You all make too much of things. I'm merely happy, that's all. There's nothing wrong with that."

"There is if it's a plain old Thursday in September. Which it is," Ruth declared as she poured three cups of cream into the electric mixer. "I know, you've finally booked one of those trips you're always talking about. Which one are you going on? The weekend in Shipshewana? The bus tour to Colorado?"

"My happiness has nothing to do with trips."

Christina Kempf, twenty-two and adorable, looked over her shoulder while she did the dishes at the sink. As usual, her white *kapp* and violet dress looked as neat as a pin. "Does it involve a boy?"

Miriam wanted to continue to play it cool, but Christina's question made her toss the rest of her resolve out the window.

These were some of her best friends. If she couldn't share her news with them, she didn't know who she'd share the news with.

"Yes," she finally announced with a broad smile. "Yes, it does. The best thing just happened when I went out to the dining room to pour coffee. It was so *wonderful-gut* I can hardly believe it."

Ruth turned off the mixer. "Well, don't keep us in suspense. Tell us!"

"And be quick about it, Miriam," Marla said with a broad grin. "I'm already imagining all kinds of things."

Miriam breathed deep. "Junior Beiler asked if he could stop by my house tonight," she blurted in a rush. "He said he has something he wanted to talk to me about."

After turning off the faucet, Christina rushed to her side. "Oh, Miriam, he's going courting!"

"I think so," Miriam agreed. "After all, why else would be want to come over to my *haus*?"

"I certainly can't think of another reason," Ruth said.

Christina squeezed Miriam's hands, her own getting covered in flour as she did so. "Junior is so handsome. He has such blue eyes, too."

Miriam nodded. Though her eyes were also blue, they certainly weren't the bright blue shade his were. "I know."

"And his hair is so blond."

"I know." She'd always thought his blond hair was attractive. Much better than her mousy brown.

"I'm not sure who he is," Ruth admitted. "Maybe I should go out to the dining room and get a good look at him."

"*Nee!*" Miriam protested. "If you go out there you'll stare at him. I know it."

"I'm not that bad."

"Yes, you are," Marla said.

Still so happy to share her news, Miriam almost squealed. "I could scarcely believe it when he motioned me over to his table. I thought he only wanted *kaffi* . . . but he wanted to chat with me!"

"I'm so happy for you," Marla said. "You've got such a good heart. I'm glad Junior has finally taken notice of you."

"Me, too," Miriam whispered to herself. Now that her big news had been shared, the four of them went back to work, Miriam still feeling like she was on cloud nine.

Then the kitchen doors opened and Jana glared at them all. "I could hear your laughter from the dining room! Just because Valerie is here to wait tables, it doesn't mean you all can do nothing in here."

Before any of them had a chance to point out that they'd been working, Jana snapped, "Whose turn is it to clear tables?"

Miriam raised her hand. "Mine, I'm afraid. I'm sorry. I'll go right out and do that."

"Honestly, Miriam, I don't pay you to come in late and stand around the kitchen chatting. I suggest you get yourself together before you lose this job."

Stung, Miriam rushed out to the dining room and hastily started clearing the tables.

Normally, the harsh words from her boss would have rattled her more. But today, nothing could spoil her good mood.

She hoped the day would fly by, since she was certain that the evening was going to be special.

At last, her life was going to change. She was sure of it.

About the Author

· · · · · · · · · ·

SHELLEY SHEPARD GRAY is a two-time *New York Times* best-seller, a two-time *USA Today* best-seller, a finalist for the American Christian Fiction Writers prestigious Carol Award, and a two-time Holt Medallion winner. She lives in southern Ohio, where she writes full-time, bakes too much, and can often be found walking her dachshunds on her town's bike trail.

Visit www.AuthorTracker.com for exclusive information on your favorite HarperCollins authors.